TEEN
ROB

08/29/24

Robinson, Stacey

Dancehall rebel

Dancehall REBEL

Dancehall REBEL

STACEY ROBINSON

JAMES LORIMER & COMPANY LTD., PUBLISHERS

TORONTO

James Lorimer & Company Ltd., Publishers acknowledges funding support from the Ontario Arts Council (OAC), an agency of the Government of Ontario. We acknowledge the support of the Canada Council for the Arts. This project has been made possible in part by the Government of Canada and with the support of Ontario Creates.

Cover design: Tyler Cleroux
Cover image: Sabira Langevin

Library and Archives Canada Cataloguing in Publication

Title: Dancehall rebel / Stacey Robinson.
Names: Robinson, Stacey Marie, 1978- author.
Identifiers: Canadiana (print) 20230541054 | Canadiana (ebook) 20230549268 | ISBN 9781459418158 (hardcover) | ISBN 9781459418141 (softcover) | ISBN 9781459418165 (EPUB)
Subjects: LCGFT: Novels.
Classification: LCC PS8635.O264 D36 2024 | DDC jC813/.6—dc23

Published by:
James Lorimer & Company
Ltd., Publishers
117 Peter Street, Suite 304
Toronto, ON, Canada
M5V 0M3
www.lorimer.ca

Distributed in Canada by:
Formac Lorimer Books
5502 Atlantic Street
Halifax, NS, Canada
B3H 1G4
www.formac.ca

Distributed in the US by:
Lerner Publisher Services
241 1st Ave. N.
Minneapolis, MN, USA
55401
www.lernerbooks.com

Printed and bound in Canada.

Contents

To the ancestors and artists who established the special musical force that is reggae, and to the generations of creators carrying the rhythms and culture into the future.

CHAPTER ONE
One Love

"Denise, you look good, girl! You coloured your hair!" my Auntie Claudia said when we arrived in Mandeville, Manchester, Jamaica. My older cousin Rohan had picked us up from the Norman Manley International Airport in his silver Toyota RAV4.

It wouldn't be a visit to our beloved Jamaica (aka *Yard*) without someone commenting on my weight, skin, or clothing within the first few seconds of seeing me ... after a hectic drive in from Kingston on the highway. "Thanks, Auntie Claudia. I missed you!" I said, fluffing my lime green-dipped curly ponytail. It had been flattened from leaning against the car's headrest.

"I missed you, my baby!" she responded, squeezing me into her thin frame with a smile. "I know you're going to have some new style every time I see you . . . your outfit, or your hair colour. Or another piercing," she whispered. "Me and your mommy have to keep an eye on you to make sure you don't go too far and get a tattoo next."

"Denise!" my cousin Shelly-Ann squealed, rushing down the stairs of her new apartment complex. "I'm so excited to show you everything in person!" she said. A new lawyer, Shelly-Ann rented the space for herself. Her brother, Rohan, was living with her while he finished his Music Education degree at Northern Caribbean University in town, and Auntie Claudia lived further into the countryside.

"I guess you don't need to stay by me anymore now that Shelly has her place," Auntie Claudia teased.

"Mommy, you're literally fifteen minutes away," Shelly-Ann said, rolling her eyes and reaching for my hand. "Anyhow, you guys will be out with Uncle Fitz and Auntie Charmaine, so Rohan and I can keep Denise company."

"True, it's just a quick visit. Next time though, you can spend one night back at the house," Auntie Claudia decided.

"Shelly Belly!" I said, kissing my cousin's cheek, and adding her to the hug with Auntie Claudia. Soon after, Uncle Linval joined in. My parents and Rohan were rearranging the bags in the car and called for me to come and get my hand luggage.

I loved to visit Jamaica and was there at least two times a year. One or both of my parents would travel, and I'd tag along when I could or when there was nothing important happening at school that week. Jamaica, to me, was paradise. Even though I was born and raised in Brampton, Ontario, Canada, Yard always felt like home.

I was ready to have an amazing time catching up on the decorations in Shelly-Ann's place, and the new music Rohan would introduce me to. The melodies, the food, the delicious scents, and being with my cousins were everything I loved about the island.

Uncle Linval was talking to my dad. "You're almost fifty like me . . . you might as well start building up a retirement house here, Fitz."

"Soon, soon," Dad promised. I knew he eventually wanted to settle and buy a second home in Jamaica, but he had been too busy to move forward with this plan, as well as being focused on paying my upcoming school fees and tuition.

My parents were a big part of the Jamaican community back in Toronto because they were so connected to the music scene on the island as well. My dad had been invited to co-host a Reggae Month launch that weekend, put on by a local restaurant in town that his old schoolmate owned. He loved this event and linked up with his friends there every winter.

Both of my parents were born on the island and had moved to Canada as young teens to live with relatives. My mom came with her Aunt Eunice, and Dad came to live with his older brother Conroy. Although I didn't have their natural Caribbean accents that had stayed with them over the decades, I loved Jamaican culture as much as I loved Canadian culture.

***

While our parents were out, we spent our time chatting, eating, and watching the latest music videos on YouTube. Every now and then, I'd catch Shelly-Ann raising her eyebrows at me, but I wasn't sure why.

She would let me know soon enough.

We were driving into Mandeville with our windows up and the AC blaring, going into the Super Plus to grab some ice cream sandwiches when I saw The Girl. Standing outside the grocery store in a pair of yellow basketball shorts, a white Lakers tee, and a matching yellow baseball cap. She had caramel brown skin and long brown locs twisted into braids that fell down her back. She was wearing a few black rings and a black beaded necklace. She had sunglasses in her hand, along with an unsmoked spliff. She was extremely pretty without trying to be. I gave her a complete scan in seconds.

"Afternoon, Sister Shelly-Ann," the girl said politely as we walked toward the entrance. She grinned. She had a beautiful-but-cute smile, and her eyes were a nice shade of brown, especially with the sun shining her way. She nodded at my cousin and then looked at me.

In those seconds, I believe we saw each other. She saw me the same way I saw her. I was wearing a lot of colour, my hair was combed back into a low ponytail, and I had been experimenting with Shelly-Ann's Fenty makeup collection. I felt cute, too. I looked away quickly, and back again. When we locked eyes, I could literally feel a pull. Serious attraction.

"Afternoon, Sister Shelly-Ann," she repeated. "Stop gwan like yuh nuh see me."

"Mmm, hi," Shelly-Ann said without looking at her, and she gripped my arm to rush me into the store and grab a basket. "No shame," she said under her breath. My eyes opened wide, and I looked around at the others in the market to see if there was something weird that I didn't see.

Now if this was a boy, I wouldn't think twice about it. I definitely knew a good-looking brother when I saw one. When we landed at the airport, there were dozens of young workers around the baggage claim, around the gates, and outside near the planes.

Dressed in their uniforms, tucked-in shirts, and work vests, they were sun-kissed, neat, and they all had bright smiles. It was hard not to stare at them, but I kept walking, while they all continued to watch.

"Enjoy your visit," they would say, cool as ever, hoping their supervisors and coworkers wouldn't see them flirting.

"Welcome to Jamaica," they would call out quietly. That always happened at the airport, or even in Mandeville. The locals could always tell you were from out of town, or "from foreign" as they called it, and they would always stop to smile and admire a fresh face while they could.

I was average-looking. About five seven, with thick natural hair that I usually pulled into a low, curly ponytail. I wore glasses with a clear frame and pointy edges. I already had seven ear piercings and was counting down the days until my nineteenth birthday when my parents would consider letting me get my first tattoo: a combination of music notes and The Master Sword from my favourite game series, *The Legend of Zelda.*

"Your acne is clearing up," Shelly-Ann said to me as we browsed the aisles.

"It comes and goes," I told her, shrugging. I never worried about my appearance much and was always prepared for the comments I'd get in Jamaica — good and bad. Sometimes I was a lil thick, but this winter I had slimmed down again. Either way, I was comfortable in my skin. Even when the girl outside had been staring at me from head to toe, from behind her yellow cap.

Most of the shoppers in the Super Plus were minding their own business, so I strolled behind my cousin looking at the familiar and not-so-familiar snacks, cereals, and other items in the clean, air-conditioned store.

We found the ice cream sandwiches my mom was craving and picked up a few other treats for ourselves. After cashing out, I walked behind my cousin so I could take another good look at the pretty girl.

CHAPTER TWO
Sitting and Watching

Dressed in a pair of jean overall shorts, a bright pink tank, and my Puma slides, I was definitely feeling the vibes when we locked eyes yet again. The girl felt familiar, without saying anything, but I knew we didn't have much time so I couldn't really start a conversation with her.

I heard Shelly-Ann kiss her teeth and call for me to hurry up so we could get back home. I gave the girl a nod and smiled a bit. She returned my smile, and winked, fidgeting with the spliff in her hands, without moving her eyes from me.

"Yuh have lighta?" a young brown man with tightly braided cornrows called out, walking over to her in a bright white undershirt — or *marina* as the Jamaicans called it

— with his fitted ripped jeans resting just below the waistline of his boxers, held up by a Gucci-printed belt.

Shelly-Ann honked her horn, so I scooted across the pavement and got into the left-side front door of her white Honda Civic.

"Soooo, why is that girl outside the store so shameful? What's the tea?"

"*Because* they caught her and this tourist dancing and wining up at Margaritaville in Negril the other day."

"Shelly-Ann. You do realize that's what people come to Jamaica for, right? To dance? Meet people? Unwind . . . and wind up?"

"But it was with another woman!" she exclaimed, lowering her voice in disgust.

"Oh . . ."

"She was kissing her neck and holding her — wining behind her like some man! Somehow a clip ended up in the hands of Jamaican TikTok, and next thing . . . it seems like the whole congregation received the DM of shame. Worse, her mom, Sister Paula, is a longtime member and it didn't take long for the video to get to her. She has practically been blacklisted from the church. At first she tried to ignore it, but then when the deacons saw the video, I guess the church made a formal request to remove them from membership. It was a big deal."

"Damn. Is that fair? Sounds a bit harsh."

"Yes! Church membership has high expectations. Especially our church: dem strict."

"But . . . how will they worship now?"

"Me no know! They'll have to stay home and watch a service online. Not allowed in our church doors, that's for sure."

"It's that bad?"

"It's worse. I mean, there's a lot more of that funny behaviour out there, but most people know to keep themselves quiet and they're not showing off or being *boasie* with it. These days though, from you see them you will know them, and they tend to hang out together . . . and people talk. A heathen dem . . ."

"Not you singing Rastaman songs to me! Stop this," I said, laughing as she parodied a reggae artist who had several tunes singing out against homosexuality. "What about that guy she was with outside? Like, does everyone in town know about the Margaritaville video?"

"Of course! You know how people in the community stay — always interested in a good story. But that guy, Sister Janet's son: he always had funny behaviour."

"Really?"

"You didn't see how him look? They say he goes both ways. Imagine that? I haven't even gone one way, and some man a go both!"

I almost gasped when she said that — it was like she was peeking into my newest romantic vibe.

"Stop this. Since when do you follow gossip, Shelly-Ann? You of all people!"

"I am a woman of God. You know this — I have always been able to see right from wrong and warn you sometimes when you can't see. Dem no like me, and me no like dem . . ." she continued to sing in her deep reggae artist voice. I tried not to laugh, because the conversation was serious. "It's not gossip. I think it's a warning or a vibe that something's not right."

"This is true. You're usually right about things."

"Exactly. So, I feel it in my spirit to tell you that whatever you're seeing, or thinking about, or whatever Canadian ideas you're trying to bring here . . . don't bother with it. I repeat: no badda wid it."

"Canadian ideas?"

"*Unnu* love follow whatever the white man does, and what they teach you in your white schools — flag raising and queer praising — and you all go along with it! I see it in our family, and I've seen it in many others. Something when you people move go a foreign. You start acting like them. The young kids have lost the Lord, and you know very well that's not the way they were raised. Even if they weren't raised in the church like us, their grandparents are most likely Christians.

So they know better. But they get caught up in that weird anything-goes Canadian lifestyle."

"That's not fair to us. We can think for ourselves. Isn't that the point of moving, though? To get the opportunities available in Canada?"

"Opportunities, yes. Evil ways, no."

"Make it make sense . . . I'm not sure if I should be offended yet," I teased. One thing about Shelly-Ann, she would do whatever it took to prove her point.

"I have my degrees from UWI, right here in the Caribbean. It's possible to be successful without leaving your home. Without having to sell out your soul or take on the British or Canadian — or the American lifestyles."

"Well, Miss Smarty Pants, since you have so many big degrees, and you're a big lawyer now, you should be able to figure out that you don't have to worry about me. You never did, and you won't have to. My parents knew what they were doing with me and have given me a lovely Canadian life, okay?"

"A true, cuz. Just wanted to speak my mind. You know me. I don't want Shanice's weirdo energy rubbing off on you. I saw her watching you . . . like *watching* watching you, and she needs to keep to herself. Dem style don't fit Jamaica at all."

"Say less," I reassured her, replaying Shanice's cute wink in my mind, as we drove through traffic back to our family.

Her name was Shanice.

***

"Mind yourself," were Shelly-Ann's last words as we hugged at the end of that February visit. It was very, very early in the morning before Rohan returned us to Kingston for our flight. "I've seen some changes in you over the weekend, and I want you to just be careful with the path you're headed down," she said.

"What path?" I said, searching her eyes.

My family usually worried about my grades (I was a B- student who couldn't seem to break through to As), or about how much time I played video games with my Canadian cousin and bestie Shane. They sometimes fussed because I spent so much time alone, and they tried to get me out more and meet new people. Otherwise, I didn't cause any problems, so Shelly-Ann's warning caught me a bit off guard.

"The way you were looking at that Janelle Monae video? The things you said about SZA's body? Gurl . . ." Shelly-Ann pressed her lips tightly and kissed her teeth. "You usually speak like that about young men . . . smart, cute, funny young men. But other girls, Denise? Never. What happened to all those NBA players and rappers you had crushes on? Ja Morant, and A Boogie, you know? Or that boy that plays for the Toronto FC?"

I usually had my eyes on a boy or two, to keep myself entertained until I was old enough to date. I often promised my mom I wouldn't have a boyfriend until I was in university and that I would focus on my studies until then.

No one had impressed me enough to want to actually date them, until yesterday outside the Super Plus.

She was right. I felt a change, too, and it was all because of Shanice.

CHAPTER THREE
Skylarking

"You good, baby girl?" Dad asked me from his aisle seat, reaching over my mom to squeeze my knee. I nodded yes before putting on my headphones to listen to my special travel playlist: some smooth lover's rock reggae that I could comfortably doze off to.

"You good, Charms?" he asked Mom.

"Yes, sir, just hoping to finish this before we land," she said, holding up the T. D. Jakes book Shelly-Ann had gifted her. Mom was always strengthening her faith in God.

It was odd. I didn't know how to feel. I couldn't get Shanice out of my mind! The Christian in me didn't know what to make of these new emotions. Shelly-Ann's parting words echoed in my head. I left the island knowing something had changed. I knew the Jamaican culture was pretty homophobic, but I never thought it would affect me personally. I had always been so deeply in love with Jamaican music and culture, mainly because I was raised in the music, *riddims*, deejays, and sound systems with my dad.

I knew all the lyrics from the great reggae singer Dennis Brown and all of the familiar beats and rhythms of the legendary music producers from back in the day. As much as I liked the hot young hip-hop artists and a few of the modern R&B singers, my family's deep love for reggae always took over every other influence.

"Turn off that nonsense and put on some Bob Marley," my mother would tease if she happened to hear trap music or new dancehall coming out of my speakers. Or my dad would turn on his own sound and drown out my music with one of his favourite reggae instrumental rhythms on loop. They didn't care to get into the new styles and instead left that for me and my cousins and our peers to enjoy.

At the airport in Kingston before boarding, I'd read an article in the local paper about a young woman and her girlfriend who were sexually assaulted and beaten to death in Montego Bay, and I couldn't help but think about Shanice. Shelly-Ann had told me that Shanice was warned to tone down her "boyish" style by many who cared for her who were afraid she would be bullied or harmed. Sister Paula thought the anger was because

Shanice rejected all of the single young men in Manchester who tried to date her, and they were offended. Confused. Tension was high in their close Christian community.

To make things worse, a few weeks after we'd left, my cousin let me know that Sister Paula had sent Shanice away from Jamaica, after being trolled and threatened by some troublemakers on her Instagram account. "She went to live in Panama City with her grandmother," Shelly-Ann told me. "At least until things cool down, or she changes her ways."

Three months after we returned from Jamaica, I still thought about her. The more I thought about her, the more I sensed things with me were changing. I knew what I felt was real, and that it probably wouldn't go away. It was like I had opened a new part of myself . . . looking at Shanice was like looking in a mirror. It was familiar and comfortable. And extremely exciting.

I wanted to talk to her. I wanted to hear her voice. I even thought about kissing her, which was a lot for me since I hadn't even kissed a boy yet. I realized I might not see her again, but the feeling was getting stronger and harder to ignore.

***

"I'm glad I live in Canada . . . I really am," I said to my viewers in our virtual *Skylarking* stream room on a rainy May evening. We had been chatting about the red-carpet fashions at the

Met Gala in New York in real-time and rating the styles. "Do you mind if I tell a story?" I asked, and was immediately met with "yeses" from the group. "When I was in Jamaica, I realized just how different the vibe is. Like, two girls our age were raped and murdered just because they were dating. That's terrible. I know we all have different beliefs, but murder? On a seventeen-year-old? A female? Not good."

I was glad that my new, small, online music community was interested in talking about social events as we listened to music together. I felt safe sharing my thoughts with them and was happy for the space to chat.

I livestreamed a few nights during the week to practice my mixing skills. I perched my laptop on my dad's studio stand, set up my camera and monitor in the basement, lit up my special ring light, and started to play for all who would listen.

ShaneDon (Mod): Welcome to the Skylarking channel: playing the best of reggae and bringing vibes for great conversation! Finish your homework and then log in with us to unwind!

ShaneDon (Mod): ROLL CALL Y'ALL! Where u from and whatz the vibe in your hometown? Is it safe for the LGTBQ+ community? Let's talk about it!

"Yes, good question, ShaneDon," I said to the audience of eleven. Shane, in addition to being both my cousin and bestie, was also the moderator of my virtual chat room. He did a great job getting people to share, talk to each other, and feel comfortable. "More on the Montego Bay side . . . or more of a New-York-Met-Gala-red-carpet vibe with bootie cheeks out and stuff?"

Skylarking had started during the pandemic when I was getting restless and bored after endless hours of gaming. I'd seen the way D-Nice was making history in the U.S., DJ-ing music late at night on Instagram live for everyone watching in quarantine, from Michelle Obama to Snoop Dogg. The chats were so fun and the connection to others felt awesome during those early dark and scary COVID days.

"Yo! Even DJ Jazzy Jeff is streaming on Twitch. I think this is perfect for us!" Shane, a fellow music lover and my gaming partner, had told me. "It's more interactive than the live Instagram sessions, and if we're already online for *Zelda*, streaming music should be easy to get the hang of."

On most nights, I had less than twenty viewers logged into my channel. Shane would log in too, and to my surprise, we had a group of listeners whose favourite music streamer out in Ottawa had to stop to focus on work and school. She'd recommended that her followers join my community after catching one of my early streams. Our community was made up of a group of mainly Black and Indo-Caribbean girls from Southern Ontario, a few in the U.S., and we quickly became friends.

It was my encounter with Shanice that made me realize I had more in common with my new community than I realized. These ladies flirted with each other openly, and it was nice to see. Even so, I had been hesitant to join in at first and found it much easier to joke with the few boys in the chat (who also identified as gay), but it all became so much fun.

This group had entered my life for a reason, and I was ready to find out why.

Dis_Gyal: u already know how atlanta is!!!!

StaminaaDaddee: exaaaaaactly, atlanta is used to us

Dis_Gyal: bootie cheeks out and more

RainbowsAndReggae: Montreal is OK . . . u just hve to keep 1 eye open sometimes

ShaneDon (Mod): Toronto is OK I guess but its definitely nottt like ATL

"Let's talk about it! That article led me down a rabbit hole, and I couldn't believe some of the violence. Not just Jamaica... like Nigeria. Saudi Arabia. Not good."

StaminaaDaddee: uganda is sooooo anti-gay

RainbowsAndReggae: the list is long ...

Dis_Gyal: imagine not being able to leave your house??

We continued to share stories while we grooved to our favourite songs. Balance. With each stream, we grew closer. We started to learn about each other's locations, interests, and other quirks that made us unique.

There were lots of rainbow emojis shared, and sometimes flirting, but it was usually a space for jokes, to catch up on celebrity news and pop culture, and to share some uncomfortable-but-funny stories about growing up with Jamaican parents (like myself), or about a typical Trinidadian auntie (like Dis_Gyal).

We always had a good time.

Dis_Gyal: My auntie said she would lash me in public if she catch me kissing another woman! But she's the first one to wine up on her girlfriends when she dey a fete .....

RainbowsAndReggae: Soca crowds defo overlook the girl-on-girl dancing but reggae music is a tricky one . . . soooooo incredibly homophobic

ShaneDon (Mod): But still sooo incredibly vibsey, right?

"That's the thing, right? I love dancehall music, but some of the lyrics are terrible!" I said, typing to search for the song requested in the chat: "Chi-Chi Man," an extremely upbeat yet extremely homophobic tune from the early 2000s that was a familiar anti-gay anthem. "I love the music, but sometimes I try not to take it to heart or get offended. I don't think we should always take it personally . . . that's what my dad would say . . ."

GamerGlam: Sometimes you be jammin hard to an old song and then listen to the words and its like . . . whoa

Dis_Gyal: Exaaaactly but the songs still sound nice. Like its hard to not like the song

ShaneDon (Mod): It's giving . . . R. Kelly vibes . . . your mind is telling you one thing . . .

RainbowsNReggae: but your body is still telling you yes???

ShaneDon (Mod): Exaaactly lol

GamerGlam: OK @Skylarking what's one thing you learned having a dad as a DJ that we wouldn't know about?

"Hmm, that's a good question," I said, while starting another song from the same artist. "I think what I love the most is how DJs can speak through music. That's how my dad met my mom. She would go to his parties, and her friends always thought he was speaking to her because he would play perfect songs."

LisaLisa23: That's so sweet <3

"Even though she was a Christian, she said she felt God in the music he played. It touched her soul. That's what convinced her to date a DJ. She also loved how he could make people happy . . . so I also love that. The power of music. My dad showed me that."

LisaLisa23: I love to hear what music means to different people

GenevaIsHere: its an addiction huh???

ShaneDon (Mod): Big time

LisaLisa23: the best kind of addiction tho

I'd tried to explain to my parents about what I was doing online, when they'd hear me talking to myself and laughing out loud from my room. But they were so used to me gaming that they never asked for details. I spent a lot of time online that spring (sometimes nightly) and grew closer to the community. I loved our chats!

In the fall, I would be starting the Business program at the University of Ottawa. My parents saw how much more time I was spending online and worried that my gaming might be a distraction. I told them I wasn't just gaming, but they still didn't get it.

My father had been a DJ since he was in high school and my mom was his number one cheerleader. She also worked as a high school secretary, not far from our home in Brampton. They were both light social media users although my mother still bounced around on Facebook to connect with old friends, church members, and family back in Jamaica. She also sometimes updated her school's social media accounts.

Dad had an Instagram account that Shane helped him with, posting event flyers, and editing his captions and hashtags. With the support of Shane's mom, my super-beautiful and super-outgoing Auntie Donna, my dad's events would go live on her Instagram account. She had a pretty good following since she was always the life of the party. And she was stunning to look at, which definitely helped. People loved to see what she was wearing and saying. I often watched from home and would feel like I was right there with them.

But as much as they all knew about Facebook and Instagram, the Twitch and TikTok conversations were always too complicated to get into. They figured those were apps for teenagers and gamers, and they didn't have the time to get to understand them.

"The child of a DJ comes with a musical responsibility," Auntie Donna used to tease me if she saw me doing (or listening to) something corny or harmful. She always had her eyes open to make sure our family reputation stayed positive — music was our family business.

Still, I tried to explain the chat features on Twitch, the social information and humour in TikTok comments, and how Shane and I communicated with teens and college kids in different cities, but . . . they all thought it was young people tings.

"I think once you and your bestie get older, you'll realize that there's life beyond that computer screen," Auntie Donna would say. Shane and I had been gamers since we were little

... we thought it was only natural that we would enjoy playing music online too.

Music was a huge part of our lives. It always had been. My father was one of the city's most legendary reggae sound men, and a clean-hearted gentleman who the Jamaican community loved and respected. Michael Fitzroy Miller was his name. He was forty-nine years old, a dark-brown-skinned slightly thick fellow with a clean-shaven bald head and neat beard. He looked like he should be an accountant or some kind of office worker from his neat appearance and buttoned-up shirts. He dressed like the church deacon, but he could also play music to appeal to any road man or young person ... he knew it all.

"Music is his life," my mom always said to me, because my father made a living playing music. He had a house, cars, and built a solid life for us through his music.

Like my mom, he grew up in the church, and we attended regularly as a family when I was younger. As the Saturday nights out became busier, and sometimes even had him travelling out of the country, it was hard to keep up our early morning Sunday routine.

During lockdown, we really reconnected and watched a lot of online services to lift our spirits and stay focused, which was nice. With events outside and finally back to normal again, the older crowd he entertained was more than ready to party, and he was number one on their list. Every weekend. Thursdays and Fridays too. Even day parties were more popular, so sometimes he'd have two events per day on the weekend.

"Run chune, Denise, my girl!" Dad would encourage me. "Juggle, Denise! Juggle!" he'd call out when I'd mix from song to song.

Sometimes when I was downstairs in the studio, I would catch my dad at the top of the basement stairs, listening to what I was playing. I would see his shadow or hear the steps creak a bit. If I did a nice mix or something special, he would slap the wall and cheer before continuing on his way to the kitchen or garage: "Yes, my *selecta!*"

He taught me everything I knew about music and watching him DJ over the years made me want to follow in his footsteps. Even if I only played music online, I wanted to help people feel good and get through the day like he did.

Streaming on Twitch truly got me through the pandemic. We'd built a small but loyal community, and it helped me to learn so much about the world . . . and about myself. I'd started to welcome the casual flirting with the other girls and became comfortable flirting back. It felt natural. I didn't question it, and no one knew but us. We were safe to just be in our little zone.

***

One evening in June before our stream, Shane was over at the house with my Auntie Donna. Shane and I were watching music videos on YouTube, and he selected an old Rihanna track.

"I would sell my laptop for just one minute in her presence," I said, boldly. It was something I'd always thought, but I wanted to see how it sounded out loud. Her skin tone and light eyes reminded me of Shanice back at the Mandeville Super Plus.

"You said the same thing about Janelle Monáe after the Met Gala." Shane chuckled.

"I did?"

"You did."

"So, if you had to choose?"

"I wouldn't. They're both so badass."

"So . . . ?" Shane looked at me across the kitchen table where we were sitting, having some grapes. "You exploring your options . . . beyond your friend Jaylen? Beyond boys?"

I started to laugh, because I knew he saw what was going on, and I knew he didn't care either way. I shrugged, and we laughed until our mothers shushed us from the living room, where they were catching up on Netflix programs. They didn't even catch the play.

We went down to the basement to livestream, knowing

that our moms would be in the living room and kitchen, snacking and chatting for hours that Friday night. My dad was napping after playing at a friend's fundraiser in Ajax that afternoon, so we had the studio to ourselves. Shane took a seat on the couch with his MacBook. I sat up on Dad's stool and set up my special green lighting.

We had only been live for about an hour when Auntie Donna came dancing down the stairs to the old classic song I was playing, "Murder She Wrote." She was a big dancer and usually the first one to kick off any event. My mom bounced down after her. They couldn't resist the music!

"What do you know about these songs?" Mom said to me, as she often did despite being the one who had introduced me to those very same songs as a child.

"You're really good, honey," Auntie Donna said, not realizing she was stepping into the camera's view with me. Shane didn't even bother to stop her. He was too busy laughing at the expression on my face as Auntie Donna two-stepped around me.

"Watch *bits a fly!*" Shane said, as the online community responded to Auntie Donna's dancing with digital donations.

ArleneTheDream: omg shes juuuust like my auntie

Dis_Gyal: Everyone has an Auntie Donna

RainbowsNReggae: Or an Auntie Janelle

Meelz: Charlene!

DannyBoi: Keisha!!!!!!!!!!

"So true!" I laughed. The names kept coming, sounding like all the names of my parents' Gen X friends.

DannyBoi: Uncle Omar!!!

Dis_Gyal: Uncle Andrew

StaminaaDaddee: Uncle Kevin.

The laughter was loud, and my mom and her sister had no idea what was happening, despite our best efforts to explain to them — again — that we were streaming. They thought we were just playing for each other, and the whole chat room and donation part was too much for them to learn.

We had a fun night. They continued to dance while Shane moderated the chat room and told me some of the comments and messages to me that I couldn't catch. The jokester DannyBoi in Kitchener was always making inappropriate comments to GamerGlam, a young lady in Ottawa, and it had become an ongoing storyline in our chat — even though DannyBoi had a boyfriend, and GamerGlam's girlfriend LisaLisa23 was in the chat with us too. It was silly but entertaining. Always.

I continued to play a selection of nineties dancehall classics that I knew our moms would enjoy and that would also bring warm memories from the chat room. I played all the greats — it was a hit, and it made everyone happy.

Reggae music was in my blood. Every special occasion in my life had musical memories attached to them. I remember the song my parents played for me on my birthday mornings when I was in elementary school. Songs that were usually played in the summer. Songs for Christmas. I was happy to be able to play for my mom and Auntie Donna, and even watch Shane get up and text from his phone while he danced himself. Shane, like his mother, loved to dance.

Music was a gift that I was sure God blessed our family with. It was the passion behind everything.

CHAPTER FOUR
If I Had the World

"Watch big sound a play!" My dad eventually came downstairs. He leaned against the wall, drinking a cold ginger ale as he watched me DJ.

Despite being from the old school, he was up to the times with his technology. He grew up DJing with vinyl records, but he was just as skilled on the digital Serato DJ software and laptop as he was with the turntables.

The stream ended after three hours, and I raided my community over to another music streamer, a Filipino brother in Seattle named RaggaMarvin who played a lot of mellow, dub reggae. My dad plugged in his laptop and lovingly nudged me out of the way to continue where I left off.

"What, you trying to have a sound clash, Daddy?" I teased

him, moving aside to see if he wanted to battle song-for-song, like we did on weekday nights after dinner before the pandemic. He started with his go-to artist, as usual. Dennis Brown. No matter what the occasion, Dad had a D. Brown to set the mood. This evening it was "If I Had the World," which had us all singing out.

I never pushed my dad's sound system to its limits in volume. I knew that was his job. As the bass hit the basement walls, I joined Shane by his laptop to review our Twitch stats and to spend a few minutes in the Seattle chat room with RaggaMarvin, respectfully.

"You're like an angel to me . . ." Dad sang out on the microphone, to my mom. She blushed and rolled her eyes as she started to clean a bit, and Auntie Donna folded some laundry she saw on the couch (that I was eventually going to get to).

It was a nice night. No big parties scheduled, so they didn't have to worry about getting ready and the whole hoopla.

Shane's dad, Uncle Randy, came over just around midnight to join my dad with a half bottle of rum. The two of them continued to play music and drink, talking about the NBA season and the latest Raptors player news. Soon, their *bredrens* Uncle Carleton and Uncle Andre passed through as well. Dominoes began to slam, and the music continued to automatically run on playlist.

Shane and I went back to the kitchen to grab another snack and decided to stay up there and chat. "What's up for this weekend?" I asked him.

"Wedding tomorrow, one of my mom's work friends. Pops doesn't really want to go, so I told her I'd follow her."

"Okay, I'm just gonna go look for some more stuff for my dorm."

"Time's moving fast, ah lie?" he said, shaking his head.

"It's true. I'm looking forward to Ottawa though."

"I need you to be on high hot gyal alert for me," he warned me.

"Wow."

"I need a nice university bae. Someone to make me a better man, you know? Smart. Cute."

"So I have to go and play matchmaker? Since when?"

"Just for out-of-town links. You know in person, I'm good. I'll handle the girls on my own campus."

"And online. I see you trying to see who's down," I teased him. Shane was always, always looking for new girls to talk to. It never failed: they were forever drawn to his big, bright eyes and baby face, his messy Afro, and playful personality.

"I can't lie, there's nuff pretty girls in the chat, you know," he said, rubbing his hands together. "If I can't touch, I don't mind looking."

"I'm telling you! Everyone's a baddie!" I agreed. "I see those profile pics!"

"What about you? You hoping to meet someone in Ottawa? I notice I haven't heard you talking about Jaylen and his little hockey videos lately? Wha gwan?"

"Over it."

"I'm shocked! You haven't talked about anything but him for the past couple years, and I thought once we were all back on the road things would level up?"

"Nah, the more I saw him — offline — I realized that most of it was just all in my head. He wasn't as interesting as I thought he was," I told Shane. "I mean, he's cute and he's such a good hockey player, but I don't think of him in any other way."

"Ah, the man gave you the ick! I thought Jaylen was gonna be your boyfriend!" Shane started to laugh. I knew he would get irritated when I would recap all of Jaylen's Instagram stories and TikTok posts to him each day. "So . . . I guess we're both going to Ottawa to look for some new baddies then?" he asked. I knew he was trying to ask if I'd be looking for female baddies. Everything had changed with the growth of our *Skylarking* community. We had both grown, in our own ways.

"You know me. If there's a vibe, I'm good," I said. "Anything goes, I guess." I didn't have to say another word. Girls or boys . . . I would give it a try and see if there was a connection.

"I thought you had a bond with the hockey kid, though. After all that?"

"I do . . . but I think the timing is off. And being in person is still awkward, after being on FaceTime for so long." Shane and I were born only a few months apart and basically grew up together as siblings. Everyone always said Shane was my twin because of how we could understand each other. We were the same height and had the same slim-ish frame. I loved Shane. He was my best friend. I told him everything.

"Besides, I bet I can get more Ottawa baddies than you," I said, challenging him with wide eyes. "Boys or girls . . . I think I have what it takes."

He smiled and reached out to give me a high five. Like Shelly-Ann, I think my cousin recognized this new spirit in me before I saw it in myself. But unlike Shelly-Ann, he was proud of me for it.

CHAPTER FIVE
Hold On to What You Got

I wasn't feeling great that morning and had been napping off and on since I woke up. Ever since our graduation ceremony and class farewells, earlier that week, my entire body shut down. Studying for exams, completing assignments, and mentally preparing to leave high school had drained me! My parents made sure I had dinner and came into my room to check on me before leaving for their friend's church banquet.

"Spinderella, you're not going to DJ online tonight for your *Zelda* friends?" Dad teased, putting the back of his hand on my forehead to see if I was running a fever.

"No, I'm just gonna chill," I told him.

My mom picked up a used plastic Raptors cup from my desk and tossed a few napkins in the garbage as we chatted.

"Well, just text if you need anything. Tonight won't be a late night," she said, rubbing my arm as she passed. "Bye, baby."

"Love you," my dad said, turning off my overhead light.

***

I was scrolling through DJ remix videos on TikTok, debating whether or not I should jump online for some *Zelda* with Shane when my cell phone rang.

"Denise, baby. You need to come meet me at Scarborough General," my mother said calmly when I answered. Something about her tone let me know that devastation had just visited us. I couldn't breathe. My mom had to repeat herself.

"Why? What happened?" I finally asked, panicking and sitting up in my bed.

"Take my car and come meet me, okay?" she said, sending me her location through WhatsApp before hanging up. "Be careful, please. But hurry."

I rushed to wash my face, throw on a bra and a pair of jeans, and grabbed my wallet before heading outside to my mom's Altima. It was mid-June but still chilly. I carefully drove down the 410, onto the 401, and east to McCowan Road to meet my mom in the emergency department.

One look at her startled, wide eyes told me all I needed to know. Dad was gone.

"Heart attack," she managed to say to me, weakly. I stared back at her in disbelief, bracing myself against a wall before sliding toward the floor. My mom grabbed ahold of my arm and pulled me upright. "He . . . we were just eating, and one of the guest preachers was talking, and at first I thought he was choking, but he was . . ."

"Mom. Oh my God . . ." My vision went dark, and when I woke up, I was seated in an empty private family room with Auntie Donna and Shane on either side of me. My forehead was throbbing, and my face felt warm.

"Denise . . ." Shane sobbed. His nose and eyes were red and sore. He couldn't finish his sentence.

"This is real?" I asked, looking around the space. Shane nodded, sadly, and didn't even bother to wipe away the tears on his face. Auntie Donna, speechless, had her head bowed, her eyes closed, and her hands folded in prayer. "Where's Mom?"

"She's with the doctors," Shane told me. "We wanted to wait for you to wake up, but we can bring you to her."

I tried to stand but ended up collapsing on the floor. I rested my head against the chair cushion and tried to find the strength to sit upright. My body shook, but no tears escaped. I slid to the ground, and everything faded to black again.

***

In the days that followed, my mother was quiet and numb. I tried to stay calm to make sure she didn't crumble. The minutes were unbearable. The reality was confusing. Words were blurred. I didn't recognize familiar faces. Mom and I floated through endless days, gripping one another tightly, while greeting and hosting a never-ending stream of church and community members at our home.

Our phones didn't stop ringing. Visitors revolved through our garage and backyard around the clock. Food continued to fill our fridge and counter, but I don't remember eating much.

"Condolences, Denise."

"Your father loved you so much, Denise."

"I'm here if you need me, any time of day or night, Denise."

"God is watching over you, Denise."

"Fitz never stopped talking about you, Denise. His one child. His pride and joy."

"Fitzroy was so proud that you were starting to play music, Denise."

"You are your father's angel, Denise."

Dis_Gyal: Shane told us what happened in the group chat. We love you. Sending our condolences

StaminaaDaddee: Love and hugs Denise . . . we are here for you

GamerGlam: condolences babygirl we all have you in our prayers

GenevalsHere: So sorry to hear about your dad I lost my dad last year and it feels like yesterday

ArleneTheDream: Condolences to you and your family

Meelz: Denise we are here for you and here with you

DannyBoi: I'm sorry to hear about your dad. Please call or text if you need anything at all. You will get through this

ShaneDon (Mod): I'll continue to stream Denise's playlist for her. Thank you all for your well wishes and messages. Our family is devastated

The music never stopped playing. Night and day. Only Dennis Brown tracks and no one seemed to mind. The notifications on my phone kept going off as my streaming community sent messages, tips, and songs to get me through the day.

CHAPTER SIX

Things in Life

"Fitzroy loved his girls. His baby girl, Denise, and his beautiful wife, Charmaine," our pastor's words continued, faintly around me. "He loved Jamaica. He loved music. He served his community, and most importantly, he loved the Lord."

The church was packed, standing room only. We also had a Zoom running and an overflow room where folks were sitting and watching on a large pull-down screen. The funeral was held at our family's Baptist church in Malton. Auntie Donna and Shane stayed close as did Dad's three brothers Uncle Junior, Uncle Conroy, and Uncle Clifton, and their twelve children amongst them. A few grandkids. Cousins. Neighbours. Church brothers and sisters. And those were the folks that were close to us. There were also other DJs, promoters, event planners, venue and restaurant owners, media personalities, and barbers. Chefs and bartenders. Men from dominoes, like Uncle Carleton and Uncle Andre. My mother's coworkers. A lot of my elementary school friends, and a few of my closest classmates from high school. My math teacher, and guidance counsellor. Even Jaylen.

Jaylen gave me an awkward wave, as I greeted him and dozens of others coming through the doors to the church hall. He opened his arms to give me a hug, and I accepted it weakly.

"I'm so sorry, Denise," he said, squeezing me and rubbing my back with his hand.

"Thanks, Jaylen," I said, taking a deep breath so I wouldn't cry before the service even started.

"I've been trying to reach you. I know it's a hard time, but I just wanted to talk to you and see that you were okay." I had been avoiding his calls, texts, and social media DMs. "I know with university coming up, we've all been going through a lot . . . and then this. This is a lot for anyone to handle. I don't want you to ever be alone, okay? You can call me. Even if you have nothing to say. Or even if you just want company. Okay?" he rambled nervously. Most of our chats had always been through text or on FaceTime. Being around him was always a bit weird, in person.

"I appreciate that," I said.

"Is it okay if I stay with you today? I can help get your food, or just be here to hold your hand?" he offered.

"Umm . . . I dunno, Jaylen. I really have to take care of my mom today," I told him, looking over at my mother and the group that surrounded her. "I don't want to leave her side."

"The same way I don't want to leave yours?" he said, looking down to the ground. "Is there anything I can do? Do you want me to hang out with you at the reception after?"

"No. I'm okay. I mean, I'm not okay, but I'll be okay soon. I think." I checked to see where Shane was. "Maybe you should go home after? And I'll call you later?" I said quickly, trying to find a polite way to tell him that I wouldn't have time to chill.

"If that's what you want, that's what I'll do," he replied. "I would rather stay here with you, but I don't want to get in the way. Especially with your family."

"Thank you, Jaylen," I said, reaching out to shake his hand formally. I didn't know how to act around him. One minute I thought I was in love with this guy, the next I couldn't even remember the butterflies he used to give me. They flew away the day I saw Shanice.

I didn't see Jaylen again for the rest of the day. It was a blur. All of the singing, the soulful Christian hymns. The kisses on the cheek from familiar and unfamiliar faces. The Bible verses being recited, the sound of sniffles. My mother and I sat quiet, holding hands in the front pew, and neither of us could look up. Too sad. Uncle Conroy poured his emotion into his words about his brother: he cried, he ran jokes, and he gave Dad the perfect tribute. One of the city's top reggae radio hosts closed the service in prayer before asking the sound man to play Dad's favourite instrumental track — the Promised Land riddim — as we exited the church.

The limo ride to the gravesite was eerie, along with the loud a capella singing of "It Is Well with My Soul" and "When the Roll Is Called Up Yonder." It sounded just like my grandfather's funeral in Jamaica the previous summer.

"We'll get through this. We'll get through this," my mother repeated throughout the day, barely above a whisper. "God is good. God is good." She didn't let go of my hand, and I felt hugs and pats on my back.

"God is good," I heard Auntie Donna say, from behind us.

I couldn't watch as the casket was lowered into the ground. I heard the tractor beginning to carry and lower the dirt once we finished our prayers and were getting ready to leave the area. Mom and I stood, frozen, with our hands still tightly locked. "God is good. God is good," she chanted, bowing her head. Afraid she would faint, I would squeeze her fingers lightly every now and then.

***

The reception at the church hall brought comforting scents of jerk and fried chicken, macaroni salad, corn soup, white rice, rice and peas, curried goat, and oxtail. There were fried festivals and fried plantains. Special chocolate cupcakes for the children, a red velvet cake, vanilla pound cake, and rum cake. The food moved quickly, and the hall smelled delicious. I didn't eat.

The music continued to play, select church-friendly reggae classics and cover songs of gospel favourites with some humming along from our guests. I sat next to Shane and continued to hold my mom's hand as we received ongoing condolences.

***

It was difficult to do even regular tasks. Regular movements and thoughts. Everything felt dark, sad, slow, and hopeless without my dad around.

Much like the previous summer when my grandfather died, we were trying to console one another, but also trying to keep each other's spirits at peace too. I prayed for my grieving parents, aunts, and uncles, and tried to be strong for my dad as he mourned his father. I recited scriptures and gave him words of encouragement throughout the trip to let him know I had been listening to his counsel and admiring his connection to God over the years. I wanted him to know that I had learned from the best and was going to stay strong.

After a few hours sitting around my Papa's house in Mandeville that day, when my cousin Rohan saw that my dad's tears were starting to affect me, he nodded for me to put on my shoes and join him outside.

"Come, let's do road." Rohan invited me out to run errands with him the day after my grandfather's funeral. I let the breeze play with my fingers and deeply inhaled the scent of the greenery and rich soil. Rohan turned up his stereo as we sped out of the community gates and revved up the bass on a new dancehall song. Slightly adjusting the treble while opening his sunroof, I could tell that he was also ready to leave the house, away from the sadness. He nodded heavily as he drove, mouthing the lyrics silently to himself, feeling the song. When it finished, he casually pressed the repeat button and allowed it to start again. I didn't mind. Slowing his RAV4 down at a red light, a group of schoolboys stood at the corner waiting for a bus or taxi to pass and collect them on their journey.

"Yes, Poppy!" one boy said, raising his hand in a gun-finger salute to the dancehall artist's voice.

"Bap bap bap," cheered his friend, similarly dressed in their dark school pants and now-untucked white button-up shirts. It was the end of the school day, and they, too, were happy to hear the music. The smallest of the group began to dance to himself.

"Jamaica always a keep, right?" Rohan smiled, looking over at me. Driving off from the light, he swayed his shoulder and scanned the street ahead for somewhere to pull up and park.

"Always!"

Walking from store to store was one of my favourite experiences in Jamaica. I loved the energy of activity, the aroma of foods cooking, the loud talking, and the familiar Jamaican people. I soaked in as much of it as I could, following Rohan in and out of the shops until his list was complete. The same song, newly released, continued to play from various speakers at various locations. The song was hot!

During our outing, there was a constant buzz of music. From the streets to the plazas, there was always someone showcasing their sound. Playing what was hot was a must, and I appreciated coming to Jamaica to make sure I could take in as much of the culture as possible. As the daughter and one child of Michael Fitzroy Miller, I had a stay on top of things!

"This country a de greatest," Rohan declared, smiling through our sorrow. I nodded in agreement, thankful for the strong Christian leadership and kind spirit of our Papa we had lost.

CHAPTER SEVEN
How Could
I Leave

The bass from the sound system in the basement was shaking the walls of our split-level Brampton home as I went up the stairs to my bedroom. It was almost midnight, and Dennis Brown's voice was still wailing, expressing the sadness we all felt. Reggae music was going to beat until all hours of the night because it was the way — the only way — my father would have wanted his funeral day to wind down.

"Denise . . . are you okay?" My mother wasn't far behind me, noticing how I tried to quietly remove myself from the gathering that began in the basement and had now moved into our backyard.

I gave her a sad stare as she entered my bedroom and shook my head. Sitting on my queen-sized bed I pulled my blouse over my head. "Mom, I can't even breathe," I said, folding it neatly and laying it on my pillow, comfortable in the cami I had on underneath. "I'm trying to process this, and trying to talk to everyone, but I can't accept any more hugs or condolences, and I definitely can't listen to any more D. Brown."

My ever-gorgeous mom, dressed in a shimmery black pantsuit, was still well held together during this never-ending day of activity for our immediate family.

Shelly-Ann came in the room too, shutting the door and sitting on my bed. She was also still well-groomed in a fitted black and red dress and a thin black sweater, protecting her golden tropical skin from Toronto's cool evening breeze . . . even though it was almost July. Of all the people in Jamaica, those in Mandeville were supposed to be used to a cool breeze, but they still reminded us how cold Canada was.

"I didn't want you to be alone." Shelly-Ann hugged me to her side and kissed my forehead. From my first steps as a baby, in our grandmother's yard in Jamaica, up to my high school final exams that I'd just finished, Shelly-Ann was always protecting my best interests.

"I'm okay." I tried not to tear up. I wanted to stay strong. "I'm fine. I just need a few minutes to recharge, and I'll come back down," I told them carefully, as "Here I Come" started to play downstairs.

"Wheeeeeel!" I heard Uncle Conroy yell out through the vents in his powerful bass voice. He hadn't held back at all throughout the day. He'd bawled as the casket closed before the ceremony, he danced during the walk to the cemetery, and wept and sang aloud as Dad was lowered into the ground. His best friend for life, an Atlanta resident now, Uncle Conroy was still Dad's number one fan.

"Oh Lord, if Uncle Conroy goes into Uncle Fitz's dub box, we're not going to sleep until sunrise," Shelly-Ann said. She was kidding, but we knew it was a possibility. "Let me go see what's going on," she added, looking down at her cell phone in her hand. "Look, Rohan a text me . . . he said Uncle look like he *wa'an* clash." She laughed and shook her head, shutting my bedroom door behind her as she left.

"I could use some rest too, honey, but I'm going to go back down for a bit. I understand you need space, but if we don't see you back in a few minutes, just know that we're coming back upstairs to see wha' gwan," my mom teased, squeezing my shoulder and forcing a smile. I was amazed at how she managed to hold herself together. She had shed tears throughout the day but continued to be a good host to our visitors and house guests. Her natural hair, braided back into a neat bun, was the last I saw of her before I allowed my tears to fall.

My cousin Rohan was right: the men were about to spend the rest of the night playing my dad's favourite recordings — dubplates, personalized by his favourite artists — and listen to his special music files, mixed in with other gems from the collection he had built over his musical career. My mom's family and dad's family back home in Mandeville got along well, and despite the terrible event, it was nice to see everyone together at our home for the first time. Reunions usually took place on Jamaican soil. Auntie Claudia mingling with Dad's brothers and their wives in Brampton was a beautiful thing to see.

I hadn't yet cried that hard all day, but once I was finally in my lair, I turned off the overhead light, turned on my green LED, and sat down before my laptop to allow my sobs to finally escape. Dennis Brown's voice had always resonated with the deepest parts of my soul to the point where even a simple tune about life could make me want to bawl.

My shoulders shook with the bassline from downstairs, and my eyes leaked as I listened to Dennis croon. "Should I." "Man Next Door." "Make Ends Meet." "Promised Land." Each song touched a different part of my heart with a memory of my dad and his friends gathered around turntables in various bass-filled venues in the city's west end, Brampton, and Mississauga.

A knock on my door stopped me for a moment, but I recognized Shane's familiar rhythm and called out for him to enter.

"*Zelda?*" he immediately asked, knowing that my nightly routine didn't ever change much.

"I dunno..." I told him, shrugging. "I'm trying to find some relief in this day... and I'm running out of options."

"There may be no easy way out of today," he said. "The best thing for you to do is maybe head back downstairs, accept everyone's support they really, really want to pour into you today... and just know that you are surrounded by love."

CHAPTER EIGHT
Bun Dem Out

My mom and Shelly-Ann weren't surprised to see that Shane had led me back downstairs. Mom looked up sadly and Shelly-Ann gave me a nod and smile while Shane moved two chairs for us to sit in the backyard and take in the music. I knew he wanted to hear some of the rare dubplates Uncle Conroy was determined to find.

The sadness slightly lifted as the music switched from Dennis Brown into some newer reggae selections. Liquor was flowing, marijuana was discreetly blowing, and the gentlemen remaining at our home (the music lovers, and my dad's closest family and bredrens) were determined to change the energy before leaving. Especially since the more religious family members had headed home.

"*Blaze di fyah mek we bun demmmm . . .*" rang out of the speakers. Shane swung his eyes over to me, searching for a reaction to the slur-filled song being played. The same song we'd played on our *Skylarking* stream . . . but in this setting, it took on a totally different meaning. Lately, everything did.

"Bun out Pride Month inna Toronto," Uncle Conroy's new girlfriend said out loud, dancing in the corner of the yard, a bottle of beer in her hand. She was just as energetic as he was.

"Not good," I said, causing a few people to look in my direction. I had been so quiet all day.

"Maybe don't play this song so loud, Uncle," Shane said carefully to Uncle Conroy, who looked at us both and laughed.

"You two are always so sensitive," he teased lightly. "Unnu protecting the fish dem?" he said. Shane and I looked at each other, with wide eyes. It was a common opinion in our family: they thought we were too sensitive about everything. "Maybe if they hear it, it will run them out of the city before their parade tomorrow," Conroy continued, clearly under his rum. "Genesis chapter nineteen. Brimstone and fire, we seh! Careful before dem turn Toronto into Atlanta."

"Just . . . be careful," Shane warned him lightly. "It ain't 2001." Always the voice of reason in our family, Shane wasn't afraid to check people and give them facts when it came to doing what he believed to be right. An upcoming political science major, I was glad he said something because I didn't have the energy to go back and forth with anyone . . . especially when Uncle restarted "Chi-Chi Man."

"Uncle Conroy," I said, folding my arms and tilting my head. "It doesn't feel right. Not tonight. Please."

"The two of you are something else," Rohan said, shaking his head from side to side. He had been crying all evening and had barely said a word to anyone. With one of Dad's Roots hoodies on, zipped up to the collar, he was also shivering slightly as it got later. "You two are always supporting each other, even when it's wrong. Since you were little. Let Uncle enjoy his music, yah man."

I didn't know what to say, and I didn't want to make the day worse by getting into a heated conversation with Uncle Conroy. I still listened to older dancehall music with anti-gay lyrics and chants. There were so many great songs with great rhythms that were classics! I listened to all of the reggae artists, even though I knew about their beliefs and the popular Jamaican opinion that male-female relationships were the only option. Period.

Jamaicans wore their morals with pride. Boldly. They loved tradition and Christianity. Rastafarianism. The culture had a lot of unspoken rules: actions, words, and beliefs . . . and you didn't want to get caught slipping on any of them. It was difficult to disagree, without your Jamaican-ness being questioned. Without feeling uncomfortable.

Because of my parents' taste in music, I appreciated the older dancehall songs more than I did the newer artists and the trap-dancehall style. It was familiar to me.

"Worse ting is," Shane whispered to me, "the song is a vibe, still."

"Right?" I agreed with him, knowing we were both thinking the same thing. It was not a great idea to blast a song like that outside during Pride weekend in the city.

What if our next-door neighbours heard? Their Pakistani-Canadian son had married an Italian-Canadian man the summer before COVID, and it would be rude to have them hear our song calling to set them on fire. Even though their own culture wasn't much friendlier toward LGBTQ+ communities than Jamaica's was, I knew the line of respect not to cross.

"I think everyone is giving Uncle Conroy a pass tonight . . . but it's always weird to play this song in public," Shane continued.

Shane was a young playboy, and he didn't judge folks for their lifestyle or have a certain type of friend. He found good in everyone — regardless of their sexual identity. Shane was all about the vibes and wherever there was music, he was there.

"Jah! Jah!" Uncle Conroy saluted the song as he sang along. He was hurting. He was hurting and finding comfort and healing in the music. Shane and I exchanged another look, knowing that we'd have to let the backyard bashing slide that evening. We'd have to 'low Uncle Conroy and whatever singing came out. He had just lost his best friend, and the two of us understood how close their bond had always been.

Fortunately, the "Chi Chi Man" song somehow merged into a Toni Braxton remix. With another look, Shane and I decided we could escape without being questioned while the aunties and uncles continued to weep to the R&B selections. I exhaled.

We chatted with the reunited sisters Mom, Auntie Claudia, and Auntie Donna in the kitchen for a bit. Shelly-Ann was giving them some updates from little drama unfolding here and there back in Jamaica with the politicians she worked with. I gave them each a hug and kiss on the cheek to let them know I was okay. Shane did the same and we went upstairs to my bedroom. I opened the laptop and let a new dancehall mix that Rohan had emailed me play.

"How you feeling?"

"I'm good. I'm glad today is over. Relieved, in a way."

"I understand," Shane said. "I hate to keep repeating myself, but I'm sorry you have to go through this. It will always hurt, and you'll always miss him . . . but it's life's journey, you know? And you'll get through this. We will get through this. Together. Uncle Fitz was important to all of us."

"Thanks, Shane," I said. "Let's talk about something else. Anything else. Please! I don't want to start crying again . . . I might not stop. Like, I was even looking forward to going to my first Pride with you tomorrow, but I think we better just stay home while everyone's in town. I don't want to upset anyone."

"Yeah, it's not a good idea to leave the house right now," he agreed.

"Especially to go downtown. Shelly-Ann would lose her shit," I told him.

He nodded sadly. "It would have been a nice little break, but you're right. They'll all give us major side eye for that one. Then they'd annoy our mothers talking about it for the next month. Well, I guess now we just stream, and get ready for university, and try to make the best of the next couple of months somehow? Try to stay strong, for Auntie Charms?"

"That's the plan."

"I have some ideas for new graphics and emotes for *Skylarking* that we can go through?"

"Perfect."

"I love you, Denise. I won't leave your side, okay?"

"I know you won't, Shane. I love you too, bro gad. Shane Don."

CHAPTER NINE
Better Must Come

I went to lie down on my bed, and Shane got up from the floor to sit in the gaming chair. He'd probably be there overnight, playing *GTA* to distract himself and to keep me company. We both knew for a fact that while most of our relatives had to return to Jamaica, Atlanta, New York, and other parts of Toronto, Auntie Donna wouldn't be going anywhere. Maybe ever. She would probably sleep in the room with Mom for the week.

The men in the backyard eventually brought the chairs and equipment back into the basement and started to close down. The music went silent, and the conversation eventually simmered as well. I wasn't fully asleep, but think it was around 4:00 a.m. when the last of the guests left, and I heard my mother lock the front door and turn on the alarm. The house was soon going to be empty. Just me and her. And then in another few weeks, I'd be off to Ottawa and she had to stay there alone.

It didn't feel right.

I heard my mom up and down for most of the night and figured she couldn't sleep either. Shane was still playing the game, with the headset on now, and I got up to use the washroom and go to the kitchen.

"It's impossible to sleep," Mom said, sniffling. She had been crying all night and didn't even try to stop her tears from leaking.

"It's giving *Lord of the Rings*," I said, knowing how much we both despised that movie. She chuckled. That was our favourite way to insult something unbearable.

"It will get easier, maybe?"

"Possibly." I sat on one of the kitchen stools and picked at a few strawberries on a fruit platter. "I could defer my acceptance to Ottawa, and stay home with you for another semester? Or forever? Apply to York and chill with Shane?"

"Denise, please! Of course not!" she said, shaking her head strongly. "You worked so hard to go to university, and I know you're excited to move on campus and start your business program. I'll be fine."

"But Mommy . . ."

"Honestly, Donna's just down the road, and you know everyone else will come keep me company if I need them to. I'll be okay."

"You sure?"

"One hundred percent. Is everything okay with you, otherwise? I know today was a hard day, but I'm hoping you can use the summer to refocus and get ready for school, you know? Do some shopping. Maybe we can drive over to Ottawa and see what's around one weekend."

"That sounds good," I agreed, giving her a hug with a deep inhale. "This doesn't feel real."

"Not at all," she said, also sighing deeply.

"You want to watch our show?" I asked, nodding over to the living room TV.

"We might as well," she said, picking up the bowl of fruit and joining me on the couch.

She automatically went to *A Different World* reruns, and we continued where we'd left off in season two. There were a few go-to shows we had, that we could watch when we really didn't feel like watching anything new. This show always made us chuckle and sparked good little conversations about campus life. My favourite was to hear my mom's high school and college stories, and about the older technologies. The TV shows were a great picture of the tales she shared with me.

She asked me about Jaylen, because everyone knew how obsessed I was with the boy, and everyone also realized that I had been silent about him for the last little while.

"He's around," I said, shrugging.

"I didn't see him today. I'm surprised."

"He came to the church, but I told him not to come by the house after."

"Why, Denise? Sometimes people just want to make sure you're okay."

"I know, but I didn't want him to get the wrong idea."

"Okay. Well, I didn't know . . . I wasn't sure what was going on."

"We were kind of talking, and now we're not. End of story," I said. "I mean, we're still friends, but . . ."

It was hard to explain because even I didn't understand where my attraction for him went. The more I spent time with him in person (someone I had been infatuated with for the past three years), the less I was into him. He definitely had a chill vibe, and he was smart, and cute. He was a great hockey player — one of a very few Black boys on his rep team, as usual — and he could really dance. His TikTok page was always a great mix of music, practice, and routines he'd do . . . on and off the ice. I think Shane hated on him because he also loved to dance . . . but Jaylen was the one with the confidence to post online. Shane would never. Plus, the dancing on ice was other level.

Jaylen was always a good person to spend time with in our online classroom chats during lockdown, and we talked and texted a lot. But we just didn't connect that way in real life. I tried, but I couldn't fully get into it. Especially after I saw Shanice and realized that the way I was looking at girls was changing. It all threw me off.

Even when I thought we were getting pretty close, I still wasn't interested in getting into a relationship with Jaylen. I went cold, he started acting weird overall, and it made our friendship awkward. I hoped that one day we could connect again and play *Call of Duty* or something like we usually did together. But not yet. He was probably as confused as I was, but now wasn't the time for me to have him around and complicate things even more.

"Well, you don't have time to worry about boys and dating anyhow. You're only eighteen, and you have your whole life ahead of you. Once you get into the groove of things at school, you can start to see if there are any young men out there that meet your standards," Mom said. "You're a cute and kind girl, so I'm sure you'll have a few options by the time you're ready to start dating. Someone that takes school serious, and someone who's respectful. Someone that loves the Lord."

"Yes, Mom," I said, leaning my head on her shoulder. She focused back on the television and pulled her feet up on the couch beside her. There wasn't any reason to take the conversation any further. It had been a long day, and the on-screen jokes and drama at Hillman College were all that we needed to get through until morning.

CHAPTER TEN
Equal Rights and Justice

It was my first September Friday night on the Ottawa university campus, and as much as I wanted to go out and try to socialize, I really wanted to put myself in the right headspace. It didn't take long to set up my camera, and green LED lighting was already trimming the tiny corners of my single dorm room. I logged on to Twitch and went live. I saw the numbers of my regular community members start to join the room with greetings and the new flashing rainbow heart emotes that we personalized for our chat.

From his room at home back in Brampton, Shane logged in and started his chat moderating duties. I wasn't in the mood to talk, so I decided to let the music speak for itself. I named the stream "Equal Rights & Justice" after one of my father's favourite songs, and let it play.

I loved the sounds of the instruments, the cymbals, and the one-drop bassline in reggae music. It made me feel my father's spirit. It made me feel like I was driving with Rohan, through the hills and winding roads in Jamaica.

The lyrics spoke to me, and I sat on my stool, keeping my glasses on to provide a slight reflection. I didn't want the listeners to see the tears forming in my eyes.

DannyBoi: Are u here in Ottawa yet?

ArleneTheDream: Time to turn uppp!

Dis_Gyal: Ottawa? I thought you all were in Toronto.

DannyBoi: We both started uni out east. Turn up time! Who's in town? Let's link after!

Meelz: For sure, let's do it!

Arlene — an Ottawa native, who was also a singer, gamer, and Twitch user — let us know the hot spots, and the spots for folks like us that didn't like crowds and too much hype. I knew that she'd be making plans for our local group to connect while Shane did his mod duties, so I stayed silent.

I wasn't sure how the mainly Caribbean *Skylarking* community would respond to my deep reggae oldies, but I gave it a try anyhow. I wanted to show everyone how much I appreciated the reggae. I wanted to go back to my roots. Back to *our* roots.

Despite the soothing organs and shuffling basslines of the songs playing, I could still hear the unserious action of my uncle, from the night of the funeral. How casually he dissed the LGBTQ+ community as though his own relatives weren't low-key members as well. There was one of my father's friends who I knew for a fact had a gay son, but I kept my mouth shut. I definitely wasn't going to out him, but I couldn't accept that Uncle Conroy mocked our concern, knowing the music could be damaging. As close as he was to his brother, I know my dad never played those songs so boldly outdoors. He knew the time and place.

I was caught up searching for songs, particularly from the new folder I'd downloaded from my father's hard drive. Songs I grew up on but had yet to really play. I went in. "Revolution" from Bob Marley.

Dis_Gyal: Reeeeewind!

StaminaaDaddee: Pull up!

Meelz: One more time!

ShaneDon (Mod): Thank u for the support everyone! Welcome!

The audience numbers continued to go up. I wasn't sure if people were sharing the stream with friends, or what happened, but I was going well beyond the few viewers I usually had when streaming at home. I saw the numbers grow close to one hundred and didn't know what had changed.

ShaneDon (Mod): Twitch has us featured on the main page right now!

Meelz: Amaaaaaaaazing!

Arlene sent me a private whisper and told me the same thing, that somehow my stream had been promoted to the home page of the Twitch platform. We were gaining dozens of new viewers and a few new subscribers each minute. I tried not to get nervous, but my hands shook a little as I searched the files and typed in artist names that I wanted to share. I kept typing, and playing, and typing, until the viewers were well over a hundred.

I saw some of my dorm mates log in, and they greeted me. I had given them a warning at our floor meeting when we moved in, that I was a music lover and might play at all hours of the night. They all seemed pretty cool with it, and some even asked for my Twitch and other social handles.

During our first week of classes, I connected with two girls who were the children of my dad's friends. We had been planning to link up since finding out we would be attending the same school. I didn't usually have a lot of girl friends, but I appreciated that everyone was looking out for me to keep me in good spirits. I felt protected and loved.

TeeMoney: Deeenise! It's Tonya from Sociology class!

YYZtoDeWorld: Denise and Arlene! Wha gwan!

LisaLisa23: Ah Montreal in the house! Welcome, YYZ

The numbers continued to climb, and I even saw my cousin get excited.

ShaneDon (Mod): Yuh gone a lil viral cuz!

I continued to play the revolutionary music that raised me. The higher the vibration I was on, the more tips came in, and the more the numbers rose. I got lost in the music and could see the chat room now filled with green hearts. I stayed in the seventies, knowing that a lot of my peers and new friends wouldn't be expecting it. Surprisingly, I seemed to attract new listeners waving Jamaican flag emotes as well.

I received a raid from a stream I wasn't familiar with, called *RootzRokReggae*, and was happy to welcome in seventy-five new listeners who seemed to be out in the UK. Arlene messaged me a bunch of excited happy faces, and I continued to play.

Into my second hour, I realized that we all needed the same message. We all craved the same sounds, and I was happy to provide it that night. My first night streaming music from Ottawa, and it was reaching out in a new way with new people.

LadyLiz: Lovin your vibe sis

"Thank you all for being here with me tonight. I appreciate you," I said softly. Most knew about the passing of my dad and had sent private messages of condolence and support along the way. "I love that we can use the music to uplift each other and keep each other company."

I wanted a powerful song to end the stream and went to Bob Marley. It made my tears fall and made me smile. I didn't have it in me to talk anymore. I just sat and watched the chat room light up with love and support. I watched my followers grow, and I read the messages of love.

TeeMoney: Every man got the right to decide his ...

DannyBoi: Own destiny!!

RainbowsNReggae: Get up, stand up! All rights! All people!

Ras-I-Kent: Wha gwan round ya??

Ras-I-Kent: I thought dis was a reggae room??

Ras-I-Kent: Jah Rastafari lives! These lyrics aren't for no funny guy and dutty gyal to sing – bun a fyah on the alphabet movement! How can you play Bob and wave rainbow flag?????

Ras-I-Kent: study yuh history

Ras-I-Kent: know yourself

Ras-I-Kent: Rastafari we seh

DannyBoi: Fight for our rights!

Ras-I-Kent: Rastafari lives! No Rainbows with Reggae!!!!!

Ras-I-Kent: Fyah!!!!

Shane quickly removed the negative comments before things got out of hand. A banner of rainbow and green hearts began to fill up the screen, and that's when many of the new Rasta listeners from the London stream saw our vibe. The numbers fell, but the screen remained bright with moving emojis.

I let the song play in full, to overpower the negativity from Ras-I-Kent, but I didn't have the energy to even say thanks as I finished up. Shane sent out a few messages for me, thanking everyone for being there, for supporting the movement, and for giving me a platform to mourn safely.

Within seconds, my cell began to ring. "Gurl," Arlene said, letting out a deep sigh. Since I moved to Ottawa Labour Day weekend, not even a full week ago, Arlene had been my most frequent — and welcoming — caller.

"What just happened?" I asked her, sitting on my stool and putting my head down. I felt a rush of heat, and joy, and sadness all at once. "I've never played for an audience that big before."

"Get dressed, I'm coming to get you," Arlene said. "I'm going to borrow my aunt's car and come bring you to this place. I already messaged everyone in the chat from Ottawa to let them know where we'd be."

Walking into the pub, we knew where our people were. A vibrant and diverse crowd of Black and brown students sat and stood, drinking, and singing along to the pandemic hit "The Harder They Fall" from a young Jamaican female artist. I shyly walked over to the group.

CHAPTER ELEVEN
Greetings

"You were amazing!"

"Welcome to Ottawa."

"They were streaming you live on the TVs," someone else commented.

The warm welcome felt great. I couldn't believe they had all been watching me.

"I loved your stream . . . I hope you make lots of money from it!" a waitress told me as she walked past, winking.

"Thank you," I said, taking a seat. Arlene gestured to pour me a glass of beer from the jug on the table, but I refused it.

"Oh, remember I'm only eighteen," I said, immediately feeling like a child for the confession. I was surprised they didn't card me at the door.

"Okay, no pressure," she said, pouring me a Coke instead. I was happy to take a sip and even placed an order for fries when the waitress came by. Looking around the table, I saw a fair-skinned brown boy with curly locks, singing along to the music as he munched on a chicken wing. He was sitting on the lap of a Black boy with neatly braided cornrows.

"Is that Meelz?" I asked Arlene, wide-eyed. Profile pics weren't always the same as the real-life version.

"Yup!" she said. "And that's GamerGlam." Arlene pointed to a pretty brown girl. I remembered her saying she was born in Guyana.

Two Black girls got up and began to dance, giggling as they twirled to the music. Arlene said they were second-year university students, like her. They all seemed so happy, and comfortable. I knew Arlene noticed my discomfort. I didn't know what to say, or where to look. Everything fascinated me, and I was excited for my first night out as an official university student.

"It's great to finally put faces to names."

"I'm telling you. This group has been so dope."

Arlene was gorgeous, dark-skinned with neat braids and bright eyes. She was helping me adjust to Ottawa already. Especially after meeting me in person at orientation, though, I felt like she may have developed a crush. I wasn't against it, but

I wasn't one hundred percent into her that way. She definitely seemed like she'd continue to be an awesome friend, though. We had been gaming for years! I was still texting Jaylen here and there and didn't know where my emotions were these days in general.

Now that I was on my own and finally in university, it was the perfect time for me to start dating and really try to connect with someone. I still thought Jaylen was a nice guy, but I didn't want him to be my first boyfriend. He had been texting me every day. Now that there was distance between us, it even started to feel like the pandemic days when we were on our phones sharing memes and TikTok videos, just feeling good getting to know each other.

As much as Arlene and Jaylen were both great people, I was still sad. I missed my dad, and I couldn't bring myself to feel anything but grief. No excitement, or butterflies. Plus, I was still learning the campus, and trying not to be awkward with the new people in my life — in person. I just wanted to take one day at a time.

Arlene reached for my hand and gave it a nice squeeze. She was happy to be around me, and it showed. I squeezed back but also pulled away and smiled. Thinking of girls as more than just friends was all new to me, but I definitely wanted to experience life without restrictions. I wanted to live in the moment and desperately try not to notice the pain in my heart, my head, and even my eyes at times. Losing my dad was beginning to affect me physically, and anything to distract me for a few minutes was welcomed.

"This is going to be an awesome year," Arlene said. "I'm so glad you and LisaLisa23 moved to town. And YYZtoDeWorld said she's gonna come visit too."

Meelz came over, crossing his legs and pushing an invisible lock of hair behind his ear as he sat down. "So, now that we're face to-face, I really want to know how you feel about DJing! Like, this is so exciting and I think your channel is a lifesaver. Honestly." His nails were neatly manicured with blue tips. "How does it feel, sis? You're so good. Ottawa can be a little bland, but I feel we can do something with what we just found here," he said, gesturing around the table. "Everyone is so positive, and such good energy. Last year we didn't have much of a vibe, but this year I can already tell is going to be different!"

"I love how the music brought us together. Music is everything," I said quietly, then took a sip of my pop. "It's like an addiction at this point. Always in the background of whatever I'm doing."

"I love it. You're so calm and cool and collected. And you're a gamer? I think that's dope," Meelz continued. "So glad all of us are here . . . in real life."

"Thank you. I appreciate it too."

"Hi, I'm Dionne," Meelz's friend said, leaning over to shake my hand. "I've been watching your stream too, but just lurking in the background with Meelz. I'm new to Twitch, but I love how down-to-earth and uplifting you are."

"Oh, thank you. It's been . . . fun."

The DJ in the pub changed the music, and a chutney classic came on that sent our table into a frenzy.

"*Nani wine!* The DJ found my request!" Dionne sang out to the chorus, walking to the dancefloor, bending his knees, and going down low. Meelz got up as well and dipped closely behind Dionne as others cheered them on. They looked cute together.

I wondered what their mothers knew, or how their fathers felt. I saw them free and happy but knew there was more to the story. Tension at home maybe? Family politics? Religious issues? I watched quietly until my fries came, then ate and nodded to the two calypso songs that followed.

The calypso abruptly changed to Taylor Swift, and the looks on the faces of everyone around me changed at once. Noses crunched and eyes rolled, but they continued to dance knowing they were fortunate enough to hear the fifteen minutes of Caribbean music, plus the time spent on my stream earlier.

"Is this a typical Friday night on campus?" I asked Tonya from my sociology class, a second-year student who had joined us after receiving Arlene's DM.

"Pretty much. Sometimes we have special events or bigger parties on campus. But for us, this is the hot spot," she said.

"You know what we should do?" Meelz said, dancing toward me. "We should have a party. Livestream on your channel, but we can get a venue too. Maybe we link up with the Pride and Diversity Club on campus? I dunno, just an idea." He raised his hands and moved back to the dancefloor, singing along with the Swifties on site.

He didn't have to say another word. I only stayed about an hour, and Arlene offered to drive me back to campus so we could brainstorm. We took a few sheets of printer paper and a couple of Sharpies and laid them across my tiny desk. Arlene wrote the words *Caribbean Pride Party* in the middle of the page in a bubble and handed me a marker.

"Let's just put all our thoughts on paper and see what we come up with," she said, pulling her long braids up into a bun so she could write without them falling in her face. I was so grateful for her already. Arlene felt like an old friend. She looked up at me and smiled. It was confident and brought out her pretty features, naturally long lashes, and cute dimple. I felt myself blush, realizing that she was into me. I was flattered.

"When did you . . . find the courage to finally come out to your parents . . . or to yourself, even?" I had to ask her. "Like, was it dramatic . . . or have you just kept your thoughts private?"

"Um, it was in the eleventh grade. After I went to prom with my boyfriend of three years. I realized I loved him, but I didn't love the idea of continuing to be with him. I told him I didn't feel like I was attracted to boys at all, anymore. And then I told my mother the same thing and asked her if she thought it was something I should be concerned about. She was very understanding. That was it."

"What about your dad? How did he feel?"

"My dad was in Barbados at the time, and we managed not to tell him what was going on. To this day, it's not something we discuss around him. He probably has his suspicions about me, but he would never ever say anything. We all like it this way: denial. We're not a touchy-feely-share-your-feelings type of family. At all."

"There are people in my family that are starting to get suspicious about me."

"Do you . . . feel like you might be gay, Denise?" Arlene asked carefully.

"Yes. I mean, I still like boys . . . but, I have also had feelings for a few girls, too, now," I confessed, drawing tiny circles on the paper. "But with my dad passing, and starting school . . . so much going on, I haven't had a chance to really, like . . . you know. It's just been all in my head so far."

"That's okay. Have you had a chance to talk about it at all? With anyone?"

"Not really. Shane, of course. And a few threats from my cousins in Jamaica, but no big conversations."

"Threats?"

"Basically, my cousin caught me checking out this girl in Jamaica and told me to watch out. My family is super Christian."

"Mine too," Arlene said, shrugging. "It's something we definitely dance around, but no one wants to really, like, speak about it in detail. They figure I'm still young and going through phases."

"Right," I said. "Do you ever feel . . . in danger?"

"Definitely not. I mean, my dad or my grandma in Barbados might be disappointed, but I don't feel like I'll be hurt in any way. Not here."

"I'm more concerned about what my family in Jamaica would think, more than my family here, you know?"

"I agree. My family in Barbados would flip. It's hard enough to talk about sex in general . . . let alone this."

"Are you . . . a lesbian or, like, bi . . . ?" I whispered. Arlene chuckled at my discomfort. "Sorry, I have just really needed to talk about this."

"It's all good, sis. I'm definitely into women. Girls only, please and thank you," Arlene said, with a smile. "I guess that means you're somewhere in the middle . . . ?"

"I think so. Best of both worlds?" I shrugged but was happy to have someone to chat with about it.

"Exactly," she said, laughing to relax me and reaching over to give me a side hug. "I hope moving away and making new friends really helps you with your healing, hon. I know you're going through a lot right now."

"Thank you. I am just taking it day by day."

Arlene checked her phone and showed me a text from Meelz. He had already put together details for the party: a colour theme, food theme, and music theme. He was excited.

"Sure, let's list this all!" I said, writing on the paper with green ink. I started listing some of the artists I wanted to play and realized that our *Skylarking* community really enjoyed the upbeat classics. I thought of some childhood reggae and calypso tunes I could play to keep everyone in good spirits. The revolutionary seventies reggae songs were great, but this event would have newer artists and a different energy. Upful vibes, that's what I needed.

Within three weeks we had everything set. We mentioned the party every Wednesday and Friday evening during our stream, and then every Friday night at the pub we made sure to get the message out . . . Well, Arlene did, while I sat and sipped my Coke. I was definitely trying to be outgoing but was still so used to sitting at home online in my comfort zone.

There weren't any formal invitations, but word of mouth seemed to be working perfectly fine for our little back-to-school jam. A few classmates even had friends coming in from Kingston and Montreal for the weekend to join us. Everyone realized how hush-hush and small our Caribbean community was and treated it like it was a sacred event. Everything had to be perfect.

LisaLisa23 and Tonya from class volunteered to decorate the venue and hand out party favours at the door from an online boutique that printed t-shirts and apparel with "love is love" and other slogans and phrases. We ordered them in red-gold-and-green roots colours to show our Caribbean pride.

"University of Ottawa, Carleton, Algonquin College, and Saint Paul U . . . we want to see you on Friday, September twenty-ninth at the Fanfare for our very special Caribbean Pride-slash-Welcome to Ottawa day fete!" Lisa said. A pretty and petite student who was born in St. Lucia, she smiled as she modelled her t-shirt displaying a heart with light blue, pink, and white stripes.

Showcasing the gear and taking photos for social media, she even went live a few times and recorded some videos for TikTok and IG. I loved the energy, and how in tune with social media and music this crowd was. Back at home, I didn't have anyone to play in that space with other than Shane.

When the event day came, everyone had a role and went right to work. We had a decorating team and the girls coordinating the t-shirts that were ordered. GenevaIsHere came in from Toronto and brought some Caribbean sweet treats — rum cake, coconut drops, gizzarda, tamarind balls, benne balls, currant rolls, and some coconut bread — for us to snack on. Even RainbowsAndReggae drove in from Montreal to meet us all in person.

It was worlds away from life back home with my parents, Shane, and *Zelda*. It felt like an entire community had swept me off my feet, and they refused to let me fall. Between classes, the streaming, and planning for the party, time was moving quickly, and was enjoyable.

"Welcome to Caribbean Pride Ottawa!" Meelz and his partner greeted everyone at the door. They were great hosts. They took names, put nametags on everyone, and even met folks at the door with Jell-O shots and party favours. They made sure everyone was comfortable, welcomed, and in good spirits.

I had a good playlist set up, so there were times when I let a ten-minute mix play, and times when I wanted to mix live. Surprisingly, I wasn't very nervous. I had been around enough events with my family that it felt natural.

With my stream on, I did my best to talk with the crowd in person and jump into the conversations with Shane online as well.

"Come dance with meeeee!" Arlene called out when one of her favourite soca songs began to play from a Trinidadian singer named Destra. I wasn't much of a dancer ... more of a head-nodder, so I held up my hand to tell her no, with a smile.

Instead, she joined me around the tables where my laptop was set up and began to dance behind me as I DJed. I allowed myself to relax enough to jam with her for a few seconds, before shrugging away shyly and focusing on my music. I appreciated her warmth, and how much she wanted me to enjoy my time in Ottawa. I reached out to squeeze her hand this time and was glad I was starting to feel comfortable with her so close to me.

As for Meelz, GamerGlam, and RainbowsAndReggae (a gorgeous six-foot Chinese-Jamaican fella with long legs and denim short shorts on), they ate! They were tearing up the dance floor and leaving no crumbs. It was electric, the familiar cultural movements, and the way these men wined their waists. I loved to see the rhythm and their joy. I loved knowing that my music was encouraging their excited behaviour.

"Jump up! Jump up! Jump and put your hands up . . ." the crowd of about eighty students sang out, before joining together in sync to do the "one foot bounce to the left and then bounce to the right" dance while cheering, "Palance!"

The singing out loud gave me goosebumps. Even the online interactions were lively. Our Pride party didn't feel political or deliberate — it just felt like a good time amongst friends. A safe space to welcome others . . . like me, new to town and really in need of support. Fantastic vibes.

Everyone on the dance floor grooved with each other. They drank and sang. They laughed, and even a few tumbled in tipsy bliss. From my position behind my laptop, I didn't even stop my happy tears from falling. I felt the spirit of my dad, providing music for others to feel good. He had done this his entire adult life and was the best there was. I wanted to make him proud and promised to always use my music to uplift people.

"Ten more minutes!" YYZtoDeWorld begged the bar manager when the lights came on to let us know that we had to start to wind down. It was almost time for their Friday night crowd, and our day event was supposed to finish at eight.

"I'm sorry, guys. This has been so fun, and you're welcome to come back any time . . . but the last Friday of the month is always our biggest night," the manager told us apologetically. "We'll plan to do this again, okay?"

I was actually a bit relieved to return to the dorm and process all that had happened. Arlene was disappointed that I didn't want to chill back at her place with a few others for the night, but I needed my alone time to recharge and breathe. I texted Shane to recap the night in the *Skylarking* chat that I missed and was surprised to see Jaylen up late messaging me as well.

Jaylen: WYD now . . . how was the party?

Denise: It was fun! The music was perfect and everyone out here is really nice.

Jaylen: So was it like a gay party? Like . . . is that what you're into now? I watched a bit on Twitch. Since when are you into all that pride stuff?

Denise: Not a gay party . . .

Denise: Well, kind of

Denise: The people I hang around are part of the LGBTQ+ ... I mean ...

Denise: We just wanted to have a party and hear plenty reggae and soca, and be in a safe space I guess

Jaylen: Thats a weird mix though no? Dancehall and homosexuals?

Jaylen: Why would a group of gay students get together and listen to music that disrespects them???

Jaylen: The newer dancehall isn't even too bad, but you know that 90s and early 2000s dancehall don't play

Denise: It's not like that

Denise: The music is ... what we know I guess

Jaylen: Is everything OK Denise?

Jaylen: Can I face time u?

Denise: Not right now ... I'm kinda tired sorry

Jaylen: OK. Do u miss me at all?

Denise: kinda . . .

Jaylen: I'm confused

Jaylen: r u talkin to someone else now? You don't really seem interested anymore . . . lately . . . ever since you got back from Jamaica tbh

Denise: I just have a lot going on

Jaylen: I know, between your dad, and moving out to Ottawa

Jaylen: sorry thats not fair of me to say

Jaylen: u have a lot going on fr fr

Denise: Big time

Jaylen: u don't want me to come spend a weekend with u?

Denise: What about school? And practice?

Jaylen: I know . . . but I miss u

A text came in from Arlene, just as I got into bed with my handwritten psychology notes and a highlighter. I was planning to read until I fell asleep. Jaylen was very sweet, but it was too much for me. There were too many things running through my mind, and I would rather study than think about them all.

Arlene: U good? Sleeping yet?

Denise: I'm good. Thanks again for all the support tonight. It was fun.

Arlene: Yeah u really brought a new energy around here. I appreciate it and I'm sure everyone else does too.

Denise: That's nice to hear. Everything is happening so fast. The channel is growing, I'm in a new town . . . I'm overwhelmed.

Arlene: Anything I can do to help?

Denise: You've already done so much, thanks gurl. Maybe we link and play some Zelda after I finish my readings tomorrow?

Arlene: That sounds good.

Denise: Kk, I'll text when I'm finished.

Arlene: One quick question . . . are u scared of me? Like, of being alone with me? The other day you seemed scared. And you didn't want to dance at all tonight . . .

Denise: Not scared. Maybe shy?

Arlene: well just so you know, out here . . . ur on ur own. No family or cousins to watch you or judge you. I hope I can help you feel comfortable and like Ottawa is your home too.

Denise: You are already.

Denise: I just keep thinking about my dad, my uncles, and the music . . . and just how much I was raised to not be . . . this way

Denise: I keep hearing my cousin in Jamaica and her voice telling me to watch out!

Arlene: We know girl. We all have that cousin. We all know how the 'man dem' think. That's why we've stuck so close together.

Arlene: it's been great. Nothing but love and cool people

Arlene: just know that there's nothing wrong with following what you enjoy, and following what feels right. Don't feel bad.

Denise: I know…

Arlene: I'm here for you k? For all of u.

I fell asleep after reading Arlene's last message, after a half hour of texting. I left Jaylen on read.

CHAPTER TWELVE
Pirate's Anthem

When I woke up the morning after the party, I was excited to tell my mother about the great stream I had, how my channel was growing, and my new friends who supported the party. I'd only told her about classes and professors so far, because I didn't want her to think I was being idle.

I was able to balance my schoolwork without gaming too much. I did all my readings and felt comfortable enough in my classes. It wasn't like high school at all. Everything felt important and expensive. I knew that my mom and dad worked hard to send me to Ottawa to get my degree, and I was not going to let them down.

I was ready to tell her about planning the party and how I had the opportunity to actually DJ in public and that it was something I hoped to do more of. I felt so comfortable, following in my dad's footsteps. I thought she would be proud.

"A back-to-school party?" she asked. "And you DJed on your own? That's great! You should tell Uncle Carleton."

"Yes," I told her carefully. "I will. It was a Caribbean Pride party."

"That's so good, I'm glad to see you following in your father's path in this way," she said proudly, then started to cry. "Shane told me your online show is doing well, and more people are tuning in. That's amazing. I'm glad you're adjusting," she added. "And I'm glad it's not interfering with your studies."

"No, it's helping me, if anything."

"So what type of Caribbean pride do you highlight? Like different islands, and foods and things like that?"

"We did the event with the campus Pride and Diversity Club."

"What's that, for international students?"

"No, it's more like a support system . . . and a few of the students I met on Twitch are members, so we decided to have fun together."

"That's nice. I'm so relieved you're getting out and socializing. I'm trying to do the same," she said. The Pride thing went right over her head, and I didn't have it in me to explain.

"Thanks, Mom," I said instead. She was so happy for me. "How are you doing, though? Auntie Donna been over there?"

"Every day," she said, sighing quietly. I knew she was about to cry again. "She won't leave my side, which is good. You know I'm used to having company. Having you and your dad gone is really strange for me. It's like we're both starting over."

"I'm sorry to leave you. I feel bad every day."

"Stop apologizing. You've wanted to go to Ottawa for university since elementary school. I was prepared for you to leave . . . him, not so much."

"I know, Mom. I'm sorry. It's like none of this is even real, and we just have to pretend that life is normal and do normal things."

"You don't worry about me. You just worry about your studies, and your music, and continue to make friends and just keep yourself in a positive headspace so you can get through the semester. Did you look around for a church yet?"

"Not yet."

"Well, you remember Carla from work? Her son goes to school out there, and he attends a Baptist church in Ottawa. It's small, and I think they meet in a plaza. I don't think they have a building yet, but I thought it would be a good place for you to grow with the church. Their youth group is very active in the community."

"What's the name of the church? I can check it out," I said. I really wanted to tell her about Arlene trying to date me. And how Jaylen missed me and probably wanted to visit. And how I was thinking about maybe beginning to date Arlene instead. But it wasn't the time to get back into that type of chatting with my mom. I just let her know I was making friends, called out a bunch of names, and didn't bother with any additional details. That was enough for her to handle.

CHAPTER THIRTEEN
Unchained

"Okay, so Rohan sent me this video from this school in their community that's going viral on TikTok where the students were having an activity day, and they were literally singing every lyric to "Chi Chi Man" out loud. Dancing. In their school uniforms, and no one thought this was inappropriate. Just openly, and they were having so much fun. I thought, am I overreacting? It's just a part of the culture, but they're not actually going to harm anyone . . . right?" I was playing *Zelda* and chatting with Shane on the phone.

Having a single dorm room was great. I couldn't imagine having someone else there to watch my life and listen to all my conversations!

"I don't know, man. I think it's just music to them. I don't think they're trying to cause harm," said Shane.

"I swear I never really thought about this before."

"Now that you're a member of the *community*, you wanna be an activist?" he teased. I knew he was kidding and that he knew how serious the topic was. "*But* I think you have to kiss another girl first to really say that you're playing on their team. Second base, at least."

"Shane."

"Sorry, I'm just being nosy. I hope you tell me if you decide to finally make this bisexual thing official."

"Shane!"

"Sorry. What do you want me to say? We've always been able to talk about everything. Why stop now?"

"*Bro gad*, I'm trying here. Trying to make this all feel normal, even though my entire world has changed."

"Well, *Skylarking* is doing great. People are really connecting, and I think your perspective — as a DJ — is needed!" Shane said.

"I know there's a lot of Black female gamers streaming, but not a lot of DJs . . . at least not on Twitch."

"I'm on, let's chat there," Shane said. Whenever he caught the vibe to go live, I just went with it. I turned off *Zelda* and set up my streaming settings. I titled the stream: *Caribbean Pride: Let's Talk About It.*

I left the camera off and put a screensaver video up of Bob Marley, shaking his locs in slow motion.

Denise (Host): Shane and I were chatting . . . do you feel that things are going to ever improve for how the Caribbean community views homosexuality?

Dis_Gyal: Good question. I think it's possible, but it will take some work.

Meelz: The Rastamen won't ever budge lol

Meelz: Especially the Jamaicans . . .

ShaneDon (Mod): There's nothing wrong with standing up for what you believe in . . .

ShaneDon (Mod): Jamaicans happen to be real vocal about it

RainbowsNReggae: I don't like how they're dealing with the new artists, the young women

ShaneDon (Mod): Agree, they are talented and may not get to grow because of mixup

ShaneDon (Mod): People think some of these young women are gay, and they don't know for sure

ArleneTheDream: its not fair to them

Meelz: I agree! some of the men won't even take a pic with them and definitely won't make music with them or even share a stage . . . its sad

ShaneDon (Mod): Its not our business just like our business shouldn't be anyone's business

DannyBoi: Factssssssss

ShaneDon (Mod): The new dancehall yutes are getting better with their lyrics . . . not violent anymore. Well not violent against gays, but definitely still violent lol

ArleneTheDream: Because they don't want to mess up their bag

DannyBoi: they know if they speak out, they might get cancelled.

Meelz: dem need dem visa to travel

LisaLisa23: The music scene has changed too . . . different topics. even hip hop. plenty drugs these guys rapping about now.

JamaicanKween: so tru. We need to have these conversations

LadyLiz: its important

GenevalsHere: Yes! Listen heal learn and grow

DannyBoi: Exactly!

Meelz: Right, trends come and go

Meelz: These new artists need to figure out their world, different from the elders

ShaneDon (Mod): music is the message.

User808: music is art

User808: there can't be any boundaries

JamaicanKween: I'm not saying either side is right or wrong. But we need to have the conversations with each other

Denise (Host): our culture is crucial, but I hate the hate

ShaneDon (Mod): So this is the place where we're going to have this conversation!

ShaneDon (Mod): growing in caribbean families, our parents are trying to hold on to the culture too

Meelz: The culture is changing y'all. U can see it on their faces when we do some weird shit they dont understand

Dis_Gyal: my mother thinks tiktok is hypnotizing me. especially the dance routines

Meelz: My dad makes me read a Bible verse with him every night before bed. On the phone.

Meelz: he doesn't trust me to do it on my own, and still wants to change me

ArleneTheDream: we're over here building

ShaneDon (Moderator): what if we just want to . . . exist? No drama

DannyBoi: Exist and run some tunes!

LisaLisa23: Yes! Exist and run chune.

ArleneTheDream: Exactly

Meelz: Let's use this space and make it our voice

Dis_Gyal: Raise up de banner!

Denise (Host): Fyah!!

JamaicanKween: Trample dem!!

DannyBoi: baaaaahahaa dwrcl!

Meelz: Deaddd wit laughhh!!!!!

DannyBoi: Why the most homophobic shit have to be the biggest songs though?

Meelz: Bangers

Dis_Gyal: Every time.

ShaneDon (Mod): Y'all are hilarious. Unique.

Meelz: Unique!

JamaicanKween: Unique!!

That word was all we needed to go into a full hour of Beyoncé and Destiny's Child, starting with "Alien Superstar." We had fun, as per usual, and I was so grateful for the innocent laughter and new friendships. I needed all the positive energy and good vibes I could get because the void my father left was going to be impossible to ignore.

***

"Do you feel like you have a responsibility?" Shane asked the next morning on the phone as I cleaned up my desk area. "Now that you're an ... influencer."

"I'm hardly an influencer."

"You know what I mean. You're not just at home now. This is the real world. Real faces. It's different now."

"I mean, it wasn't really something I thought about, but now, it's hard to ignore. I have a platform which is cool."

"You come from a strong legacy, my girl. We come from strong people. We should be motivated to do something like this: share music with messages."

"We should ..."

"I'll be here, regardless. I'll defend you if I have to. I'll stand with you to show everyone else that it's not that serious. It's just life," Shane said. "Yo, let's link Rohan and see what he thinks. Just generally."

We called Rohan on conference call to chat about the latest music, what was hot on the streets of Jamaica, and our usual topics. The three of us had always been close when it came to talking about pop culture and keeping each other up to date on trends.

Rohan gave his honest opinions about the current popular YouTubers and bloggers we brought up, and he told us about some videos he saw on TikTok. He reminded us that Jamaican pop culture moved so fast, and how lucky we were to have him to update us.

We took that moment to officially introduce him to *Skylarking* and send him a link. He wasn't familiar with Twitch but promised to check out the platform and prepare to log in for our next stream. He scrolled and searched as the conversation continued, but when he found his way to the names of our past streams, he became obviously bothered and soon made up an excuse to come off the line. For the first time in my life, I felt tension from Rohan that I wasn't prepared to deal with.

"I had a feeling it would go this way," Shane concluded.

CHAPTER FOURTEEN
It's Me Again, Jah

"It is true?" Shelly-Ann demanded the next morning on a WhatsApp call.

"Is what true?"

"Me hear seh you a lesbian."

"Oh my goodness! What?"

"A true?"

"No comment."

"Denise! Yuh father body not even cold yet."

"Shelly, that's not nice!" I said. Tears began to fall, immediately.

"I'm just saying, you know how he feels about . . . those things. Not to mention Grandma and Papa."

"Okay, back up a minute. What did you hear, and what are you trying to say?"

"I saw something on Shane's status. You were playing music, and I saw some rainbow flags flying in the background."

"Oh, Shane posted the stream. He always does. That's not new."

"WhatsApp, Facebook, everywhere."

"What did he say that was different? Was there a caption? How did you go from zero to lesbian like that? Didn't we already have this chat in February?"

"He said proud of my cousin-slash-bestie."

"Okay, so how did you take it so far?"

"Proud. Pride. Isn't that what they say?"

"Shells."

"Honestly, Denise. What is going on? I wanted to say something, but I know it's a hard time for you. I know you're not okay, so I'm not going to ask if you're okay. But I do want to ask you what's going on. Something has been . . . swinging in that direction in you for a while now. I've been praying for you. Every night."

"Praying for what?"

"For you to meet a nice young man, and for you to fall in love, and get married, and build a family. I'm praying for you to have the life and family you've always wanted."

"I wouldn't say I always wanted that."

"You did, you were always a romantic when you were little.

You won't remember, but we do. Ask your mom. And you loved to sing Whitney Houston with her."

"Okay, but all little girls are like that. I'm eighteen now . . . it's not the same."

"Do you want to talk about it? Have you talked about this with anyone yet?"

"Shane."

"Okay, well, can I pray with you? Is that okay?"

"Yes, sure . . ." I closed my eyes and waited to hear the gaslighting. Shelly-Ann was my older cousin, so I took her prayer/lecture gracefully and respectfully.

"Amen," she finished, after begging the Lord for my strength and clarity.

"Amen. Thank you, Shelly, I know you care."

"I do. I care about you, and Auntie Charms. Especially about Uncle Fitz, because I would hate to see you disgrace his legacy. You're lucky no one knows you're feeling this way, Denise. These older Jamaican men, especially the Rastamen. They will never let you disrespect Uncle Fitz like that. Even the Canadian ones."

"Wow . . . I don't even think it's their business, to be honest. How would they even know?"

"I know how you are, and by next week you'll have a same-sex partner, and you'll be loud and proud," Shelly-Ann said. "You foreigners move quick."

"Oh, come on, Shells. Have you ever even seen me date *anyone*?"

"What about that ice hockey boy?"

"Jaylen's just a friend."

"Well, I am calling you before this gets to Auntie Charms and before it hits the family. I know you're playing your music, but just *mine* yourself. You may think you're inside your room playing video games with a few of your online friends, but this will go international in seconds and Uncle Fitz's bredrens and their sons will see, and you know how Rohan is already. He'll interpret things in one hundred ways."

"Rohan don't miss a beat," I said, hoping to get a laugh from my cousin. It worked, but she still was stern with me.

"I'm serious, Denise. I'm not gonna tell you twice. You pray about it, you get this mess out of your head, and you read your Bible until you're seeing straight again. I love you," she said, ending the call.

I was in shock. I didn't know what to say or do. I had the phone in my hand, and it began to shake. Was God trying to tell me something? Did I deserve this scolding? It didn't feel right. It didn't feel like love.

I collapsed onto my bed. I cried like I cried the night of the funeral. It was like opening a new wound, just as the first one was healing. I couldn't breathe. I was shivering and confused.

The greatest joy I had felt since my dad's passing was now somehow turning into a family scandal.

I turned on my laptop and decided to play some gentle reggae melodies and selected an older Rastaman who created beautiful songs. I got down on my knees and sobbed into my mattress. The song was soothing, and my spirit yearned for the bass. It was the only thing that felt good, the bass travelling through my chest and skin. The track was on repeat and played over and over again. *It's me again, Jah, as I fall on my knees today . . . Help me, God, I pray . . .*

My ancestors had been speaking to me and raising me since I was a child. The music had shaped me. The rhythms had developed me. It was all I knew. Even without my dad there. With my mom four hours away. It was still my comfort and my guide.

Shane called at just the right time.

"I can *not* with Shelly-Ann," I told him, wiping my tears. We instantly both began to laugh.

"Shelly-Ann no easy at all," he said, hollering. "I'm sorry, Denise. You and I both know this is ridiculous. She's literally a virgin. Wait until she meets a man she likes, one day."

***

Shane and I always knew how to turn a bad situation around. I remembered a few weeks back in the summer, Auntie

Donna and Shane had a small barbecue at their house during Toronto's Caribbean Carnival weekend at the beginning of August. It was to say bye to me before heading to Ottawa and also to congratulate Shane as he prepared to begin his political science program at York University.

Instead of cooking, Auntie Donna catered the food and hired a young DJ to play, one of Dad's friend's sons. We shared photos and reminisced for most of the afternoon until the domino table came out in the late evening and a few guests started dancing.

"Hey, Denise," Jaylen said, walking directly to me when he entered the backyard. Jaylen's uncle happened to be friends with Shane's dad, my Uncle Randy, so I wasn't that surprised to see them show up together.

We casually chatted about school — he was heading to Brock University in the fall on a hockey scholarship — and how we weren't ready to go yet because our last couple of years were so broken up because of COVID. We felt like we could use another year or two of just being high school students. A little bit more freedom and outside time.

He was cute, in good shape, and although he was a super athlete, Jaylen was a little nerdy, like I was. We usually had great conversations. As much as Shane often teased me about him, he knew he was talented and saw the attention he was getting in the local sports media.

Jaylen tried everything possible. Told me he wanted me to be his girlfriend. Asked me if I'd ever had sex (I hadn't), or if I wanted to (I wasn't ready). He asked me about moving, and if we were going to stay in touch. For as long as I knew Jaylen, he was always hinting at things, but never really coming out and saying them. But it was August, and since we'd both be moving away, there was no time left for him to play shy.

He tried to joke around and dance with me at the barbecue. My mom and Auntie Donna saw us and smiled. They were hoping I'd start to show interest in something other than my video games and hanging out with Shane . . . while playing video games. When Jaylen started to dance, they grinned and left us alone.

Even my dad's friends 'lowed me. Probably because Uncle Randy's bredren Dwight was a well-known soccer player in the community, and they knew about Jaylen's skill as well. They let us talk. Everyone was kind, and respectful that I was healing . . . and mourning, and "extra" sensitive.

When Jaylen was going out for a quick smoke at the front of the house (away from his Uncle Dwight), I followed him and we went to walk around the neighbourhood instead. While he vaped, he tried to hold on to my hand a few times, but I casually shrugged away.

"I know it's been hard for you, without your dad. But I want you to know I'm here for you, okay? Even from St. Catharines.

Anything you need, just call," he reminded me. He was a sweet boy. Respectful. Definitely cute. "I'll wait for you to heal. I won't pressure you. I can go slow," he promised.

I wanted to cry. He was such a good friend and a great person, but I knew that my heart wasn't feeling him the way he seemed to be feeling me. And that was all I'd thought about for so long . . . being around Jaylen and getting closer. Even though he was smart and tall. Attractive and talented. He was really a nice boy, but I just couldn't.

When he stopped to check his vape cartridge, I found myself standing closely in front of him, admiring his perfect nose and cheeks. Brown skin. His earring. I took in his face and smiled at how handsome he was. He would have no trouble meeting girls on his new campus. All the girls in our school knew he was serious about his studies, focused on training for the NHL one day, and quiet, so they didn't treat him like they treated the other boys. He got a lot of respect because he always was so well-behaved. He had discipline. He didn't even let anyone else know that he smoked. Just me.

"I want to kiss you," he said, after putting his vape in his pocket. Before I could respond, he bent slightly and kissed me quickly, lingering for a few seconds without movement. It felt good. And then he gave me one more short kiss before continuing to walk. "Time's running out, and I don't want to regret not doing something before we move."

I was in shock. It was my first kiss. He pulled the vape back out as we circled toward my house. Both of his parents smoked, and he had picked up the habit now too. He said he was going to quit as soon as he moved into the dorms and started training.

"Okay . . ." was all I could say. I was confused. Excited, but confused.

"You good, Ms. Denise?"

"I'm good."

"You ready for Ottawa? Or is Ottawa ready for you?" he kidded, trying to break our new physical tension.

"I'm ready. I'm gonna miss my mom, though," I confessed.

"Me too. My parents are already sad."

"I can't believe it's time for university. Like, I feel like we all just started high school. Did high school even happen?"

"Sort of," he laughed.

We continued to walk and broke away from the awkwardness. Back at Shane's place, we played *Call of Duty* in the basement. No one was surprised — they knew how I rolled and since I was usually playing with Shane, they didn't really question my male company. My mom passed me with wide eyes a few times. She thought Jaylen was adorable and was happy to see me socializing. Shane and one of his girls joined us shortly after, and we decided to watch YouTube videos instead, chat, and eat popcorn.

When we got home, my mom asked if Jaylen was my boyfriend. She was disappointed when I said no, and I wondered why it hit her so hard. She was expecting an answer from me. She hugged me nonetheless and saw me off to bed before she returned to her room alone, watching television until she fell asleep. That was in August, and looking back, I think she already knew.

CHAPTER FIFTEEN
One Blood

After Shelly-Ann's revelation, shit hit the fan. The talk of our family was how I didn't like boys and I'd moved to Ottawa to become a lesbian. She probably said something to Auntie Claudia, and one thing led to another. It was out of hand, and my mother was beginning to buy into the hype. We chatted on the phone, but she was tight-lipped and really didn't ever get to the heart of the issue. Instead, she made plans to visit the campus for the weekend.

I was looking forward to spending time with her while many of my classmates and dormmates went home for the Thanksgiving holiday. I was ready to take a break from my studies once I caught up on my reading and assignments. My mom arrived on a Friday evening. She'd booked a hotel near the Rideau Centre, to breeze out from Toronto for a few days. She missed me!

We went out to eat, went to the mall, toured Parliament Hill, and took some photos. We had visited Ottawa once before, but it had rained during our entire trip and we didn't get to enjoy the sights the way we wanted to.

Before we knew it, our wonderful weekend—complete with a casual Thanksgiving dinner at Swiss Chalet—was over. I entered the car with my bag after spending time at the hotel, ready to head back to my dorm on Monday evening.

"How can you betray your father's legacy like this? All for musical attention?" she said, catching me off guard.

"Whoa. Where did that come from? You sound like Shelly-Ann."

"You know what I'm talking about. All this gay pride business."

"You should know I don't even like attention, Mom. It's not about that. I am just a music lover. You know that. Dad knew that."

"This is more than just playing music, Denise. It's way more, from what I hear," she said.

"But I haven't changed or done anything different. My audience was always there, and I've been trying to tell you guys about this for months. There's a community forming and it's wonderful."

"I thought this was a video game community. How did it turn into this?"

"Just naturally. Real recognize real, I guess. We all came together online."

"You kids and this Internet. It's ridiculous."

"Well, we didn't have many options the past few years. This is just how we vibe!"

"But this isn't about the pandemic. This is about who you are becoming. What's going on, Denise? Is this because of Dad?"

"No, it's not because of him at all. It's just because the streaming is getting into other spaces. Otherwise, this would be all in my head, and no one would know!"

"But you know how our people are, Denise. They will see you and see one rainbow flag, and it's a wrap. Especially the Rastamen dem."

"I'm sure when you were growing up, your parents didn't approve of *them* . . ."

"That's not the same thing. That was a different time." Mom sounded more stern than usual. It had been years since she'd spoken to me this harshly.

"Exactly. It's a different time. You can't blame us . . . it's just one of those things."

"No, you all are just out of order. This is not the way our

God created us to be. Don't you want a husband? Children? This is too much."

"I think you're overreacting, Mom. I'm literally eighteen."

"What about Jaylen? He's a nice boy. Comes from a nice Christian family. His mom is very sweet. I don't understand. Do you only like girls now, all of a sudden?"

"I like good energy, Mom. Good vibes."

"*Energy*? Oh boy. Look, I love you and you know I support you, but I'm not going to encourage this. Maybe you're going through a phase, or just finding yourself now that your dad's gone. Maybe by the time you go to class for a few more weeks, and meet some new students, you'll realize this was just an experiment or something."

"And what if I don't?"

"We'll cross that bridge when we get there. There's enough going on right now, I can only take one crisis at a time."

"This isn't a crisis. I'm okay. I mean, I'm not totally okay, but the people I've met here are great. Even Shane thinks so."

"You and Shane would defend each other through anything."

"He's coming up for our event."

"What event is this?

"The campus GSA is having a social, and they want me to DJ. We're going live and everything, on the big screen."

"That sounds good. What's the GSA?"

"Gay Straight Alliance."

"*Lawd Jesus.*"

"Mom!"

"Denise. Come on. I couldn't even tell Donna what's going on. She would lose it."

"That's what Shane said. She definitely wouldn't understand."

"I'm trying, but I don't think it's right. I can't support this, Denise. I'm sorry."

"It doesn't have to be a big deal. I'm just trying to enjoy school and feel connected," I told her, fighting to keep from crying. "I've been through a lot too, you know. My first year of university wasn't supposed to be grief."

"Then why are you making it harder on yourself, baby?"

"I'm just doing what feels good. Going where I feel comfortable. I'm going where I feel God."

"Don't bring God into this, Denise."

"Am I not a child of God? Haven't I always been? You don't think I'm praying at night for you, and for Dad, and for the family? Mom, I'm still me."

"I don't know about that," she said under her breath.

"That's not fair. I'm just trying to cope, like you are."

"No, I think you're probably causing more of an upset than

any good. The next time I come up here, I hope you snap out of this."

"Mom! Snap out of it?" I said, letting my tears drip. She'd never spoken to me this way before, and it stung.

"Yes. Please just concentrate on your studies, and don't be out here in Ottawa making a spectacle with the Gay Alliance. Join a Marketing Club or something related to your studies . . . why bring . . . sex into the spotlight?" she said. My mother sighed and quickly put her head in her hands. She took another deep breath. Our visit was ending horribly. "Look, I'm going to hit the road before it gets late. I love you, but this is going to make me cry. And *Jah* knows, my heart can't take any more tears right now. I don't think I have any left."

"Don't cry, Mom. Please."

"Just . . . know that you can stick to the music. The art. Everything else need not be mentioned or entertained, you know?"

"Mom."

"Some things just aren't natural, baby."

"What planet do you live on?" I said, calmly. I'd always thought my mom was so open-minded and accepting.

"You're already a Black woman, now you're going to add a whole other layer of problems in your life. And so much unnecessary attention on the Internet."

We both sighed, silently agreeing to disagree, but at least we weren't sobbing or mourning and reminiscing about Dad. The wound was still too fresh. This was still somehow easier.

***

Shane: WYD

Denise: Shane stoooop thisssss. U know I hate the WYD more than anything

Shane: Kidding. I just wanted to let you know I'm coming to Ottawa on a special flex. Of course I'm coming to see you . . . but . . .

Denise: Yay! What's the flex?

Shane: I met a ting online and she goes to your school. I said perrrfect.

Denise: I figured it was a girl lol. So I guess u really did get a baddie at my campus before me

Shane: IKR

I was so distracted for most of the week in class, trying my best to focus on my reading and assignments and not worry about the trouble I was stirring up in my family. My mom still called and texted every day as usual before I went to class and in the evening before bed. She seemed short with me. I had never, ever felt this level of tension between us.

That Friday, Shane arrived in Ottawa and rented an Airbnb for the weekend, inviting me to come and chill with him and his lady friend. The girl he'd met was surprisingly a very quiet and smart, cute chocolate girl. He was usually into the giddy and pretty type, but something in him seemed to be changing lately, too.

I smiled at him as he chatted with her. Shane was an amazing person to talk to, and could talk for hours about any topic and keep it interesting. I saw the look in her eyes as he spoke, and knew she was seeing the good in him that I had always known and loved.

Shane encouraged me to invite some of our *Skylarking* community over. There were seven of us at the rental in total, and Arlene was happy to be amongst us. She sat closely beside me on the couch, drinking beer and enjoying Shane's story-telling in real life. I was getting more at ease around her, and she made sure not to pressure me or make any advances. We had reached a level of comfort in our friendship.

Of course, our gathering turned into a livestream once the music turned up and Shane realized I had my equipment with me. We decided to play some new dancehall, and the conversation turned to how much we would enjoy hearing particular artists perform live.

"Did you guys go to Caribana this year?" Arlene asked the group, in general.

"The bois were out there this year! They were out in full force in Trinidad *and* Jamaica carnivals this year, too. Nuff," Meelz said.

"Nuff!" Arlene agreed.

"I liked to see it though," Lisa said. "It's nice to see more men in costume."

***

We'd gone to Caribana that past summer, Shane and I, on a music mission. We had been a few times as children with our parents, but it was our first time going downtown on our own. We took the GO Train from Brampton to the Exhibition, and were immediately caught up in the mood of the parade. We heard the latest soca music pumping from various trucks along the way. Costumed masqueraders gathered and prepared for a day of music and jumping up on the streets, overlooking Lake Ontario.

"This is fantastic," I said.

"I agree."

"You can literally feel the bass."

"Look how happy everyone is!"

"I don't remember it feeling like this when we were kids."

"Not even close. It used to seem so confusing. So loud."

"And now that's what we want: loud and confusing!" I laughed, and it felt good.

We wandered through the crowds, listening to conversations as the parade got underway. We walked with the costumes, with the spectators, the tourists, and security. We grooved to the rhythms and swayed to the live DJs. We were both in our element, listening carefully to see who had a sound that we liked.

Most of the parade was predictable: trucks playing music, girls in costume, and a few men dancing with them. Water bottles, sweat, and pure joy. There were so many emotions as we walked through the parade and then back up to the street to eat and catch the train back home. Shane and I hadn't said much, but I think we both felt the weight of the crowds and how powerful our people felt when there were so many of us gathered together.

It had been hard for me to play music for a few days after the Carnival. I was inspired. I felt alone. I missed my dad. I loved the DJs on the parade route. I wanted to absorb all of that energy and keep it with me for one of my down days. I played a lot of *Zelda* and a little bit of *GTA* to distract myself from feeling so deeply sad and so extremely happy at the same time.

CHAPTER SIXTEEN
Never Give Up My Pride

It became more difficult to juggle my business classes, learn (and remember) so much new information, and still find time to stream and play my games. Even Shane seemed to be busy with his studies, and as we headed into November, I realized that I needed a plan to balance everything. Especially the hobbies I needed to help me get rid of my stress.

When I returned to *Skylarking*, I decided to be very clear with what I said and how I said it. I wanted to really help everyone else get through their tough times too.

"I grew up listening to the greatest reggae music. They sang about love. Truth and justice. I grew up with this music in my soul . . . so right now, as much as I want to hide and maybe even stay in bed and avoid my problems . . . I'm going to keep fighting . . ." was how I started my stream. "I've sent this link out to my family members, knowing that they may not like what they see, but also knowing that this is the way my dad expressed himself, and I am finding my peace through these same songs. I want to share my peace with you guys. I know I don't usually talk this much, but it's been on my mind. Thanks for listening."

ShaneDon (Mod): Type in the chat, tell us the craziest thing your Caribbean parents have said to you . . . and how you clapped back

Meelz: Mom said I was a sinner

StaminaaDaddee: Adam and Eve, not Adam and Steve. Her fave.

VinylCityPA: My dad hasn't talked to me since 2019.

DannyBoi: My uncle said if he didn't know me he would light me on fire

ArleneTheDream: OMG, he's a Ras?

Meelz: Obvi

DannyBoi: Of course

ArleneTheDream: Fire tho?

DannyBoi: Fyahh!!

"Well, music has brought me through my good times and bad. I grew up on these artists. My dad loved Dennis Brown, which is where I actually got my name from. So . . . my go-to song is "Make Ends Meet" whenever I'm having a hard time. My dad would listen to it on repeat. I can still hear the needle and the sounds of the records. The bass. After his sessions . . . he would always seem to feel better. What song does that for you? What song growing up provided you with comfort . . . and continues to inspire you?"

DannyBoi: I actually love to hear the old Rastaman tunes from the 90s . . .

ShaneDon (Mod): Jah Jah City!!

ArleneTheDream: I love the lovers rock

Dis_Gyal: Big chunes! Someone Loves You Honey

ShaneDon (Mod): Classic

"Keep sending in your requests, I appreciate you all listening in," I said, taking a sip of water. I didn't want anyone to pity me. I didn't want to have to go online to complain about all the reading I had to do or how much I missed my dad. I tried to stay strong and continued to play the songs requested in the chat.

ShaneDon (Mod): Yooooo, it was so nice to see everyone in person the other day

ArleneTheDream: nice little community, eh? IRL

ShaneDon (Mod): I agree . . . I'm sending Denise all the requests. So when they get played remember to screen record us, save us, share the live, share the music . . . and use #MoreLife #SkylarkingFam

Meelz: You want us to be public public, huh?

ShaneDone (Mod): I just hope we can reach other people who might need a space like this to unwind.

"Real talk though, do you all still dance to the homophobic songs?" I asked, hoping to lighten the mood.

Meelz: Every time

ReggaeNRainbows: Bangers

DannyBoi: Chi-Chi Man? A banger.

DannyBoi: Log On? Banger.

ArleneTheDream: Should we laugh now or cry?

Dis_Gyal: Neither . . . we dance! And maybe play some soca instead?

ArleneTheDream: OK run some Patrice for us!

ShaneDon (Mod): Type in your requests, guys. Let's turn the energy around in here.

Meelz: Appreciate you Denise!

CHAPTER SEVENTEEN
Queen Majesty

I was happy to be back in Brampton again. Even though the Christmas break was approaching, I didn't mind popping home for the weekend in November when I heard that my classmate Tonya was heading that way for a couple of days. My mother and I decided to spend the Friday evening together alone, and we planned to eat with Auntie Donna, Uncle Randy, and Shane the following evening. On Sunday, I would drive back to Ottawa with Tonya.

"You know I haven't played any music since you moved away. No one has come to ask either since the funeral. Do you want to string up the sound?" Mom asked.

"Of course! Let's eat dinner down there."

As we ate Greek take-out that we ordered as a treat (we

loved souvlaki!), my Mom retold the story of when she met my dad. It was a long weekend event for Caribana in the early 2000s, and everyone was dressed in army print. It was a reggae dance called the Soldier's Ball, a popular event each year.

"Mom, did you ever used to like ... *skin out* and *wine up* on the dancefloor, back in the day?" I teased. It was a question I had always wanted to ask her but never had the courage.

"Denise!" she said, laughing out loud. She hollered, and it sounded so sweet. I'd missed that laugh.

"You know, like in those nineties' videos? Women wining in those bright wigs, or wearing those leather batty rider shorts?"

"Me? Never!" my mother gasped, raising her hand to her chest as she continued to chuckle. A tear fell from her eye. She was happy. "I was so innocent!"

"I'm gonna ask Auntie Donna. I know she was dancing on her headtop for sure," I concluded, laughing at the thought.

"Donna was always the dancer. I was like . . . her hype person, but I usually was a bit more shy. Same way you see us now was how we were back in the day. Same with Daddy. He was always a cool cat."

"No one could shake him."

"Right. He commanded respect, wherever he went. Even when he wasn't playing music. As popular as he was, and well-liked, you couldn't really over-hail or over-greet him or be too hype around him. He didn't like that."

"That's why you guys were a good fit. Fun . . . but serious."

"Exactly."

"Who do you think I'm most like?" I asked.

"That's hard to say. You have the best parts of both of us. You're kind and soft-spoken . . . like me. But you also love music and have an ear for melody like your Daddy."

"I agree. I think we're all pretty laid back, though."

"Yes. People always said that about us. That we were simple. Humble. But don't get it twisted. You know your dad could also defend himself any time, any place. Me too."

"Oh, I know that much! I think that's how I've fallen into this role . . . with my *Skylarking*." I took a breath. "I know it's hard for you to understand, but in some weird way . . . this is the best way for me to express myself. And heal. And help others do the same. This is me doing exactly what the music trained me to do. Defend myself."

"I know. I know, and you're right." She sighed, knowing where the conversation was going. "But . . . some of the things you're fighting for. It's . . . it's not the Christian way to go about life. And it's okay to be quiet sometimes. Not everything has to be in-your-face."

"I know."

"For example, you know how your dad used to speak to me through music? He let everyone know there was a special lady that caught his eye. I knew it was me," she said. "Sometimes you can make your point without being so out there . . . or loud, you know?"

Mom grew up in Malton and was a Christian, but after her mother passed away back in Jamaica, she moved out of her Aunt Eunice's home, and started to party more and hang out around Toronto's reggae scene with her more rebellious sister, Donna. That was when she met Dad. Always a very pretty lady, she was an attention magnet. Men were always trying to talk to her, but she was so innocent. Only nineteen.

Daddy played so many songs from the singer Monica that night because everyone said Mom looked like her. I think it was the slow jams that got her. "For You I Will." And then "Why I Love You So Much." "Before You Walk Out of My Life." "Angel of Mine" was the song that caught her. This was 1999, and a very big hit. Apparently, it *buss* the dance, because people realized Daddy was talking about a real girl. In the room. It sounded and felt like love, and he didn't care who knew!

My family loved to tell this story, those who were there. And how Mom's friends dragged her up to the DJ booth after the party, in the name of love. Especially Auntie Donna. She had so much respect for Dad because she said he had a good heart. People often spoke about his clean heart.

He'd asked her to dance when the party was winding down. They talked all night and didn't stop . . . until that awful day in June. I couldn't imagine how empty my mother's heart must have been, missing her first and only love.

"Why don't you go live on your show now? Let me see?" Mom asked, surprising me.

I moved quickly, took out my laptop, and set up my usual lighting. The first song I played was for my mom, "The Boy Is Mine." Just to make her laugh again. Monica's voice sang out.

StaminaaDaddee: You love the 90s huh?

Denise (Host): Its my parents fave

Meelz: Same

I continued to play songs I knew my mom liked, and I even told her to come on camera with me. "It's my mommy, everyone!" I said, kissing her cheek. She did a little shimmy and then leaned into the microphone.

"Hi, everyone! We're just having our own pre-Christmas

party tonight." Running her hand down my arm she said to me, "Go ahead, let me see how you do the whole operation."

ShaneDon (Mod): Hey Auntie Charms!!

"Shane's saying hi, Mom," I told her, pointing to the chat. The few listeners online filled the screen with hearts and smiley faces for her to see.

"Hey, Shane!" she said, stepping back into the camera for a moment to wave.

I continued to play some nineties R&B songs that I knew she loved while Shane moderated the chat room. I usually gave him a heads-up when I was going to go online to play music, but he was pretty good about dropping what he was doing to come in and support once the notification hit his phone.

It was the best I'd felt since my dad passed. Listening to the oldies in my socks in our basement, grooving as my mom sipped her tea and sang along. After the stream, I collapsed on the couch, smiling. It was so much fun to have my online friends and my mom there. Especially being around my dad's system.

We let a Whitney Houston album run from beginning to end. Mom went upstairs to get some chocolate cake for us to share. Each bowl had a scoop of Oreo ice cream.

"Okay. Honey, I can see this channel and sharing the

music for your friends makes you feel good," she began slowly. "But the family is really worried about you. Every day someone brings it up to me. It's almost at the point of harassment."

"Then don't answer them," I said simply. "They've always been more hype than you. Calm and humble, right? Don't let them draw you into the drama."

"Denise, I can't do that," she said. We didn't have much time left together, and neither of us wanted to leave the way we had the last time. "Especially if we . . . well, if you are the drama. I feel so unsettled knowing that so many people around us are being spiritually burdened by this."

"Mom. Their spirits don't have to worry about mine. I have my own relationship with God, so they can rest," I said. "You need to stop letting Auntie Claudia and Shelly-Ann call you and stress you out!"

"So," she said carefully after a moment. "The chat room seemed pretty innocent."

"It's all innocent. It's our fun. Sometimes it's like our therapy," I said. "For real. What did you think we were talking about?"

"Oh, I don't know. Everyone's been filling my head with the worst-case scenarios and sending me articles about young women being attacked . . ." she trailed off.

"Mom."

"Is anyone pressuring you to do anything or be anyone you don't want to be?"

"Mom, you know the answer to that."

"I know," she said with a deep breath. Then she took a few more deep breaths. "It's been a really, really hard couple of months."

"I agree."

"I just can't handle anything more to deal with."

"Me neither."

"I don't want you to ever feel like you can't talk to me."

"Thanks, Mom."

"And I want you to know I'm here for you."

"I know," I said again, reaching for a bottle of water. "But you don't have to bring Auntie Claudia and Shelly-Ann and everyone's opinion into our lives. Now that dad's not here, they have more of your time, and they're going to keep pushing."

"Girl, I'm just about ready to leave the family group chat for a little bit. It's too much. Every day. Hearing the sadness in everyone's voice notes. Over and over again. The pity. The scriptures, and old photos, and so much gloom and worry! It pains me."

"For real."

"I mean, I don't mind our other chat group with Donna

and Shane, but the big group chat with Linval and Rohan and them? Too much."

Before she finished her thought, I picked up her phone and deleted the WhatsApp family chat group from her device, handing it back to her with a grin.

"Done and done. It's OK for you to take time to yourself to heal."

"Denise," she said, smiling at me. I knew she was trying not to cry. "I don't want to bring you any stress. Not now. Not ever. I just want you to live a happy life."

"Thanks, Mom," I said again and smiled, knowing that was all I could ask from her. "I know."

"But I can't deal with *this* right now. Definitely not over the Christmas holiday. Maybe not even next year. Maybe never . . ." she began to sob, softly. "I need you to promise me that you'll find a church this month with a youth group, or maybe volunteer with the Sunday school or children's program. Can you do that?"

"Of course."

"We've never had to deal with this in our family before," she said carefully, trying to control her tears for my sake. "And now is not a good time," she added, firmly. From her delicate emotional state, I knew that it was best to leave it alone. I would let Shane know, and we'd have to carefully adjust our conversations and movements online.

As I continued to get comfortable with my new friends, my growing platform, and my out-of-town routine, I'd have to find a way to be myself and hopefully still discover my first romantic relationship. I'd continue to share my music and promote positive vibrations. And I'd always find a way to protect my mother from any more harm. That's what my dad would want, too.

I understood my assignment and had been preparing for it my whole life.

Acknowledgements

To my family, friends, and teachers who encouraged and supported my storytelling and writing activities over the years: I appreciate you!

Thank you to Allister Thompson and the team at Lorimer for believing in my work and providing me with this special opportunity to share my writing with young readers.

— *S. R.*

From the Author

This book is rooted in a love for music while looking at how this love can intersect with contradictory values, beliefs, or religious practices — across cultures. I hope this story can serve as a source of reflection, awareness, and a catalyst for conversation. Denise's family represents many parents, cousins, or community members of all backgrounds who are unsure of how to navigate unfamiliar lifestyles or technologies. This story can be a tool and example for those who need to explore these changes across generations, as Denise approaches her new reality with respect for her family and the culture she was raised in while nurturing her independent journey into adulthood.

— Stacey Robinson, 2024